The People vs Friar Laurence,

The Man Who Killed Romeo and Juliet

Book by Ron West
Music and Lyrics by
Phil Swann and Ron West

A SAMUEL FRENCH ACTING EDITION

SAMUEL FRENCH

FOUNDED 1830

NEW YORK HOLLYWOOD LONDON TORONTO

SAMUELFRENCH.COM

ISBN 978-0-573-69740-1   Printed in U.S.A.   #29183

RENTAL MATERIALS

An orchestration consisting of **Piano/Vocal Score** will be loaned two months prior to the production ONLY on the receipt of the Licensing Fee quoted for all performances, the rental fee and a refundable deposit.

Please contact Samuel French for perusal of the music materials as well as a performance license application.

IMPORTANT BILLING AND CREDIT
REQUIREMENTS

All producers of *THE PEOPLE VS FRIAR LAURENCE, THE MAN WHO KILLED ROMEO AND JULIET must* give credit to the Author of the Play in all programs distributed in connection with performances of the Play, and in all instances in which the title of the Play appears for the purposes of advertising, publicizing or otherwise exploiting the Play and/or a production. The name of the Author *must* appear on a separate line on which no other name appears, immediately following the title and *must* appear in size of type not less than fifty percent of the size of the title type.

THE PEOPLE VS FRIAR LAURENCE, THE MAN WHO KILLED ROMEO AND JULIET, was produced by David Castellani at the Tamarind Theatre in Los Angeles on January 16, 2004. The production was directed by Ron West, the musical director was Phil Swann, and the orchestra was comprised of Phil Swann, Ron West, and Rick Hall. The stage manager was Josh Miller. The cast was as follows:

PRINCE ESCALUS. . . . . Rick Hall

FRIAR LAURENCE . . . . Bruce Green

SAMPSON, Capulet's kinsman. . . . . Nicole Parker

GREGORY, Capulet's servant . . . . Michael John Ross

ABRAHAM, Montague's kinsman . . . . .Joe Zanetti

BALTHAZAR, Montague's kinsman. .Beth Crosby

BENVOLIO . . . . Sarah Gee

TYBALT. . . . . Michael John Ross

LORD CAPULET. . . . . .Hal Lublin

LORD MONTAGUE. . . . . David Castellani

ROMEO. . . . . Norm Thoeming

MERCUTIO, ROMEO's friend . . . . David Castellani

PARIS, a rich bachelor. . . . . .Joe Zanetti

JULIET. . . . . Nicole Parker

THE NURSE . . . . Bruce Green

LADY CAPULET . . . . .Beth Crosby

AN OFFICER OF THE LAW. . . . . David Castellani

SERVING WENCH. . . . . Sarah Gee

FRIAR JOHN . . . . Sarah Gee

MRS. GIBBS. . . . . .Beth Crosby

MR. WEBB. . . . . Michael John Ross

ANOTHER CAPULET SERVANT . . . . David Castellani

AN APOTHECARY. . . . . Michael John Ross

ASSISTANT APOTHECARIES . . . . Beth Crosby & Nicole Parker

EXECUTIONER. . . . . Sarah Gee

THE PEOPLE VS. FRIAR LAURENCE, THE MAN WHO KILLED ROMEO AND JULIET, was produced by Second City Theatricals (Andrew Alexander, executive producer, and Kelly Leonard, Robin Johnson, and Joyce Sloane, producers) at the Chicago Shakespeare Theater (Barbara Gaines, Artistic Director and Criss Henderson, executive director) on Navy Pier in Chicago, Illinois on May 14, 2004. The production was directed by Ron West, with costumes by Alison Siple, properties by Keith Hoop, casting by Bob Mason, and scenic and lighting design by Heather Graff & Richard Peterson. The musical director was Phil Swann, the conductor was Lisa McQueen, and the production stage manager was Jennifer Matheson Collins. The cast was as follows:

PRINCE ESCALUS . . . . Rick Hall

FRIAR LAURENCE . . . . Bruce Green

SAMPSON, Capulet's kinsman . . . . Nicole Parker

GREGORY, Capulet's servant . . . . Brian Gallivan

ABRAHAM, Montague's kinsman . . . . David Castellani

BALTHAZAR, Montague's kinsman . . . . Roberta Duchak

BENVOLIO . . . . Lauren Ashley Bishop

TYBALT . . . . Brian Gallivan

LORD CAPULET . . . . Ron West

LORD MONTAGUE . . . . David Castellani

ROMEO . . . . Keegan-Michael Key

MERCUTIO, ROMEO's friend . . . . David Castellani

PARIS, a rich courteous bachelor . . . . Rick Hall

JULIET . . . . Nicole Parker

THE NURSE . . . . Bruce Green

LADY CAPULET . . . . Roberta Duchak

AN OFFICER OF THE LAW . . . . David Castellani

SERVING WENCH . . . . Lauren Ashley Bishop

FRIAR JOHN . . . . Lauren Ashley Bishop

MRS. GIBBS . . . . Roberta Duchak

MR. WEBB . . . . Brian Gallivan

AN APOTHECARY . . . . David Castellani

ASSISTANT APOTHECARIES . . . . Roberta Duchak & Nicole Parker

EXECUTIONER . . . . Lauren Ashley Bishop

CITIZENS, SERVANTS, PARTY GUESTS, MUSICIANS . . . . . The Ensemble

HOW TO DO THIS PLAY

It takes 9 actors (6 men and 3 women) to do *THE PEOPLE VS FRIAR LAURENCE, THE MAN WHO KILLED ROMEO AND JULIET*. There is a little leeway in the doubling, but **BENVOLIO, FRIAR JOHN, THE SERVING WENCH**, and the **EXECUTIONER** must all be played by the same woman. **TYBALT** and **GREGORY** must be played by the same man. The **PRINCE** must also play **PARIS**. See Appendix 2.

I like to cast a blonde woman, a brunette woman, and a redhead so the audience can never get them confused. I want the audience to identify them by hair color at intermission. If you have a budget for really great wigs, forget I said anything.

Do the play in modern dress. I don't want there to be jokes about guys in tights. See Appendix 3.

The gag props (the flowers, the bear, et al.) must be actual items, but the masks and the swords are, in the manner of improvisational theater, space work items. This saves you having to rehearse with actual swords. It will also save money. See Appendix 4.

The **OFFICER OF THE LAW** who first appears in Scene 18 is a very specific characterization. You might want to substitute the alternate scenes detailed in Appendix 1.

The whole thing flows best if you have a lot of entrances. In Chicago we had 9. Generally, when a new scene begins, the lights change, but it is incumbent on actors in the new scene to take focus. For instance, Romeo starts Scene 13 before the women in Scene 12 have left the stage. If you want to try the show with no light cues, I say go for it.

Yes, *THE PEOPLE VS FRIAR LAURENCE* contains some indelicate language, attributable to Phil Swann's rock and roll roots, my background in anarchic improvisation, and Shakespeare's original text, which, occasionally, is beyond ribald. In deference to the standards of schools or communities wishing to produce *THE PEOPLE VS FRIAR LAURENCE*, Appendix #6 contains author-approved alternate lyrics and dialogue.

I put Juliet's chamber right and the dungeon left. Mantua was far left. I used the center for street scenes and the Friar's cell, which is where Friar Laurence lives and ought not to be confused with the dungeon.

Above Juliet's chamber (audience left) I had a star field in the shape of The Big Dipper. Above the arch in the center, there was a wooden cross. Above the dungeon was a copy of the sculpture "The Lovers," adorned by floating hearts. Star, cross, lovers...get it?

Ron West
March 15, 2006

ACT ONE

1. INT. DUNGEON

(The piano tolls an ominous A minor figure as house music fades and lights go to black. Lights up. **FRIAR LAURENCE** *sits on a wooden bench, the prisoner of* **PRINCE ESCALUS**, *his inquisitor.)*

PRINCE. You're in a lot of trouble, Friar Laurence.

FRIAR LAURENCE. I'm telling you, Prince Escalus. I'm innocent.

PRINCE. And you're not helping yourself with crazy talk like that.

FRIAR LAURENCE. It's the truth, Prince.

PRINCE. You killed Romeo and Juliet and now you're trying to cover your tracks.

FRIAR LAURENCE. I made every effort to do the right thing. Last summer, I tried to keep the peace between their families.

(Lights change.)

2. EXT. VERONA, A PUBLIC PLACE

*(***GREGORY** *and* **SAMPSON** *enter jauntily and sing #1, "It's a Beautiful Day in Verona.")*

GREGORY & SAMPSON.
IT'S A BEAUTIFUL DAY IN VERONA,
THE ITALIAN CITY STATE.
GREGORY.
I'M GREGORY.

SAMPSON.

I'M SAMPSON.

GREGORY & SAMPSON.

OF THE HOUSE OF CAPULET.
IT'S THE MONTAGUES WE HATE!
WE ARE OFTEN DRUNK OFF OUR ASSES[1]
'CAUSE PURIFIED WATER IS SO SCANT.
WE BRAWL IN THE STREET
BECAUSE THE PRINCE IS TOO CHEAP
TO BUY A SEWAGE TREATMENT PLANT.
IT'S A BEAUTIFUL DAY IN VERONA.

GREGORY.

WE'RE NOT THOSE TWO GENTLEMEN OF LITERATURE.

SAMPSON.

WE'RE MERELY SIMPLE SERVANTS OF OUR LORD
CAPULET.

GREGORY & SAMPSON.

WE CAN'T READ OR WRITE OUR SIGNATURE.
IT'S A BEAUTIFUL DAY IN VERONA.
THAT WE KNOW FOR SURE!

(**ABRAHAM** *and* **BALTHAZAR** *enter, pushing the
others out of the way.*)

ABRAHAM & BALTHAZAR.

IT'S A BEAUTIFUL DAY IN VERONA
IN THE SIXTEENTH CENTURY.

ABRAHAM

I'M ABRAHAM,

BALTHAZAR.

I'M BALTHAZAR,

ABRAHAM & BALTHAZAR.

AND MONTAGUE'S OUR BOSS.

ABRAHAM, BALTHAZAR, GREGORY, & SAMPSON.

YOU'RE OUR MORTAL ENEMY!

(*They all draw swords.*)

---

1 See Appendix 6 for alternate lyrics and dialogue.

UNLIKE THE KILLING OF KING HAMLET
WHICH LEFT ALL OF DENMARK ROTTEN,
THE BASIS OF OUR QUARREL HAS BEEN
TOTALLY FORGOTTEN.
AS DRUNKEN STUPID LOUTS
WE HAVE FIN'LY FOUND OUR NICHE.
TO INSULT EACH OTHER'S MANHOOD,
WE CALL EACH OTHER "BITCH."[2]

(They trash talk and have a sword fight for two bars.)

FOR IN THIS DAY AND AGE,
FRAILTY IS WOMANKIND
AND IT'S A BEAUTIFUL DAY IN VERONA
IN THE GOOD OL' SUMMERTIME.

(They fight again. **ABRAHAM** *drives* **GREGORY** *off-stage though we can still see the latter's arm through the next swordfight.* **BENVOLIO** *enters and sings the bridge.)*

SAMPSON. It's Benvolio!

BENVOLIO. That's right, and in the name of the house of Montague, I demand you…

(sings)

CEASE THIS SAVAGE FIGHTING.
ACT AS EUROPEANS DO.

ABRAHAM.

I'LL THROW GARBAGE OUT THE WINDOW.

BALTHAZAR.

I'LL EXPEL SOME JEWS!

BENVOLIO.

I MEAN, REFRAIN FROM VIOLENCE
OR YOU'LL ANSWER TO MY SWORD!

ABRAHAM.

THAT'D BE FINE WITH ME,
I'M LIKE FIFTEEN AND REALLY BORED.

---

2 See Appendix 6 for alternate lyrics and dialogue.

(There's another sword fight for two bars. **TYBALT** *enters. All partake in a brief hip-hop homage.)*

BENVOLIO. What, ho, Tybalt!

ALL BUT TYBALT.

WHAT HO, TYBALT! WHAT HO, TYBALT!

TYBALT.

THERE IS NO GREATER MENACE
THAN A SWORD THAT'S HELD BY ME.

ABRAHAM.

UNLESS YOU COUNT THE PLAGUE
WHICH IS SPREAD BY RATS WITH FLEAS.

ALL.

WE'RE YOUNG AND DUMB, WE THINK WE'RE HUNG,[3]
WE'RE VIRILE AND WE'RE TOUGH!
WHEN OUR HONOR IS AT STAKE
WE DON'T SHY FROM FISTICUFFS!

(They fight for two bars. **ABRAHAM** *is driven off-stage.* **FRIAR LAURENCE** *enters.)*

FRIAR LAURENCE.

WHAT IS GOING ON HERE?

TYBALT.

OH, GREAT, IT'S FRIAR LAURENCE!

FRIAR LAURENCE.

I'VE GOT TICKETS FOR THE CARNIVAL
JUST LIKE THE ONE IN FLORENCE.
IT'LL BENEFIT THE UNDERPRIV'LEGED
KIDS HERE IN VERONA.

EVERYONE ELSE.

PARDON US IF WE DON'T CARE.

FRIAR LAURENCE.

YOU'RE DRUNK!

TYBALT.

YES, ON CORONA.

---

3 See Appendix 6 for alternate lyrics and dialogue.

ALL BUT FRIAR LAURENCE.

WE'RE YOUNG AND RICH AND BORED AND
PRE-DISPOSED TO BEING JERKS!
WHO GIVES A SHIT ABOUT THE POOR
OR DOING VOLUNTEER WORK!?[4]

(Two bars of fighting. **LORD CAPULET** *enters.)*

CAPULET.

WHAT IS GOING ON HERE?

TYBALT.

HELLO, LORD CAPULET.

*(***LORD MONTAGUE*** *enters.)*

MONTAGUE.

WHAT IS GOING ON HERE?

CAPULET.

MONTAGUE!

FRIAR LAURENCE.

AND I WOULD BET
THAT YOU EACH WOULD BUY SOME TICKETS.

CAPULET.

I WOULD RATHER HAVE SOME WINE.

MONTAGUE.

NO, THANK YOU, I AM LOOKING FOR THAT
LOVESICK SON OF MINE.

(Lights feature **ROMEO** *far left.)*

ROMEO.

I'LL PINE FOR ROSALINE
LIKE A CORPSE CRAVES A TOMB.
ASSIGN SWEET ROSALINE
TO CUPID'S CLASSROOM.
SHE'S THE ONE I'M THINKING OF.
IF MUSIC BE THE FOOD OF LOVE –

(Lights change, **ROMEO** *exits.)*

---

4 See Appendix 6 for alternate lyrics and dialogue.

MONTAGUE.

ON SECOND THOUGHT, FORGET THE KID.

ALL.

EN GARDE! YOU CROSSED THE LINE!

*(**PRINCE ESCALUS** enters.)*

PRINCE.

WHAT THE HELL IS GOING ON HERE?

EVERYONE ELSE. *(kneeling)*

IT'S THE PRINCE, OUR NOBLE LORD.

PRINCE.

YOU'VE BEEN FIGHTING IN THE STREET.

EVERYONE ELSE.

WE'VE BEEN PLAYING SHUFFLEBOARD.

PRINCE.

VERONA IS DERIDED

IN THE WHOLE OF ITALY.

I CAN'T LURE THE TOURISTS HERE

IF YOU BEHAVE SO BRUTALLY.

I DEMAND TO KNOW WHAT HAPPENED HERE,

COMMAND YOU TO COME CLEAN.

FRIAR LAURENCE.

SURE, LET'S JUST GO BACK TO THE

BEGINNING OF THE SCENE.

*(All ad lib their enthusiasm as most scatter and exit. **SAMPSON** stays on to begin recapping for the **PRINCE**. The others re-enter in quick succession.)*

SAMPSON.

IT WAS A BEAUTIFUL DAY IN VERONA.

I WAS WALKING WITH GREGORY.

WITH CHIPS ON THEIR SHOULDERS,

THESE TWO GOT BOLDER.

ABRAHAM & BALTHAZAR.

HE BIT HIS THUMB AT ME!

BENVOLIO.

THEN I APPEARED AND SAID, "HEY, BE CIVILIZED!"

TYBALT.

BUT THAT ONLY LED TO A SWORD FIGHT REPRISE.

ALL.

'CAUSE WHEN TYBALT GETS INVOLVED
IT SHOULD BE NO SURPRISE
THAT EVERYTHING GOES WRONG!

(**ABRAHAM** *exits.*)

FRIAR LAURENCE.

THEN I ARRIVED AND ASKED FOR PEACE.

ALL.

THAT LASTED FOR FIVE SECONDS.

CAPULET.

THEN I CAME ON

MONTAGUE.

AND I CAME ON.
OH HARKEN, MY SON BECKONS.

(*Lights feature* **ROMEO**.)

ROMEO.

STILL PINING FOR ROSALINE
I FEEL I SHALL SWOON.

ALL.

YOU'RE YOUNG, BLAH BLAH BLAH BLAH BLAH.
TIME HEALS ALL WOUNDS.

(*The* **PRINCE** *kicks* **ROMEO** *offstage. All but* **FRIAR**
and **PRINCE** *kneel.*)

FRIAR LAURENCE.

AND THEN THAT SILLY PRINCE APPEARED–
OH SHIT, WHAT AM I DOIN'?[5]

PRINCE.

GO NO FURTHER, FRIAR, OR YOU'LL
BRING YOURSELF TO RUIN.
I HEREBY PUT MY FOOT DOWN
WHICH MEANS I DO DECREE
THERE ARE FOUR THINGS THAT
DO DEFINE VERONA, ITALY!

---

5 See Appendix 6 for alternate lyrics and dialogue.

(Ritard. The music has a stentorian feel.)

ALL.

ONE.

PRINCE.

KNOCK OFF THE FIGHTING IN THIS
FAMILY RIVALRY.
IF YOU DON'T YOU ARE SUBJECT TO
A QUICK DEATH PENALTY.

ALL.

TWO.

*(**ROMEO** enters.)*

ROMEO.

FATE DETERMINES ALL
IN AFFAIRS OF THE HEART.
IF YOU ARE STAR-CROSSED LOVERS
YOU'RE DOOMED RIGHT FROM THE START.

*(**ROMEO** exits.)*

ALL.

THREE.

CAPULET & MONTAGUE.

MONTAGUE HATES CAPULET.
THERE CAN BE NO ACCORD.
WE JUST DON'T HAVE A CLUE
TO WHAT WE'RE FIGHTING –

ALL.

– FOUR!

IT'S A BEAUTIFUL DAY IN VERONA.
WE OUGHTA MAKE THIS TUNE OUR CITY SONG.
IT'S A BEAUTIFUL DAY IN VERONA!
WHAT COULD POSSIBLY GO WRONG!

*(As they hold the last note, **ROMEO** enters into the middle of the group.)*

ROMEO.
> STILL PINING FOR ROSALINE!
>
> *(Blackout.)*

3. INT. DUNGEON

*(Lights up. **FRIAR LAURENCE** and the **PRINCE** as before.)*

PRINCE. That was your big effort to keep the peace. Selling tickets to a carnival.

FRIAR LAURENCE. It was the first of many efforts I made to ease the situation. You were there, Prince. You know their families were bitter enemies.

PRINCE. Here's a photograph of Capulet and Montague. They're shaking hands and embracing. Do they look like enemies to you?

FRIAR LAURENCE. This "photograph." Where did you get such a thing!

PRINCE. Da Vinci invented it.

FRIAR LAURENCE. It's unbelievable!

PRINCE. Shut up and answer the question.

FRIAR. It's well known the families are bitter enemies. This "photograph" must have been taken at the tomb after the kids died. I should know, I was there –

> *(The **FRIAR** bites his tongue. The **PRINCE** sings #2, "Trouble.")*

PRINCE.
> OH, YOU'RE IN TROUBLE. YOU JUST ADMITTED
> YOU WERE AT THE SCENE OF THE CRIME.

FRIAR LAURENCE.
> WELL, THAT PROVES NOTHING.
> THERE IS A FUN'RAL MASS
> THAT I INTONE AT TOMBS ALL THE TIME.
> FATE WAS THE CAUSE OF POOR ROMEO'S DEATH
> AND THE CULPRIT IN THE YOUNG GIRL'S DEMISE.

PRINCE.

> DO YOU REALLY THINK VERONA WILL SWALLOW THAT?
> EVEN CHILDREN TELL MUCH BETTER LIES!
> OH, YOU'RE IN TROUBLE IF YOU ARE SAYING
> ALL THIS HAPPENED BECAUSE GOD DOESN'T CARE.

FRIAR LAURENCE. I'm not saying that!

PRINCE.

> IF YOU CONFESS NOW BEFORE THE TORTURE,
> WE CAN SKIP TO THE ELEC-TER-IC CHAIR.
> MAYBE CAPULET WANTS TO THROW THE SWITCH,
> MONTAGUE COULD THROW A PARADE.

FRIAR LAURENCE.

> WHAT IN THE WORLD'S AN ELECTRIC CHAIR?

PRINCE.

> IT'S ANOTHER THING DA VINCI JUST MADE!

> (**FRIAR LAURENCE** and the **PRINCE** speak over the
> score.)

FRIAR LAURENCE. I'm telling you…one thing led to another…uh, inexorable fate caused the demise of Romeo and Juliet.

PRINCE. But you believe in Jesus and all that. What happened to free will, huh?

FRIAR LAURENCE. God's will trumps free will.

PRINCE. Sounds like somebody's making it up as he goes along.

FRIAR LAURENCE. You have to believe me. I tried to help the boy.

(Lights change.)

4. INT. DUNGEON/FRIAR LAURENCE'S CELL – FLASHBACK

*(The song continues as **ROMEO** dashes on and kneels to the **FRIAR**'s left. With a foot in each reality,*

the **FRIAR** *is interrogated while simultaneously hearing* **ROMEO***'s confession.)*

ROMEO.

FRIAR, WON'T YOU BLESS ME, FRIAR?
I'VE GOT SO MANY SINS TO CONFESS.

(spoken)

Friar, I was not as good to Rosaline as I could have been.

FRIAR LAURENCE. Forgive yourself, son. She was not the girl for you.

PRINCE.

FRIAR, WAS IT WORTH IT, FRIAR?
WHY DID YOU MAKE SUCH A MESS?

FRIAR LAURENCE.

AS LONG AS YOU SAY HAIL MARYS EV'RYDAY AND
OUR FATHERS TO THE OMNISCIENT—

ROMEO.

MY HEART'S IN A VICE.

PRINCE.

NICE TRY, BUT NO DICE.

ROMEO & PRINCE & FRIAR.

MERE PRAYER PROVES TO BE INSUFFICIENT.

(Lights restore. **ROMEO** *exits.)*

5. INT. DUNGEON

(The **FRIAR** *and the* **PRINCE** *speak over the score.)*

FRIAR LAURENCE. No, prayer is the answer!

PRINCE. If you don't get what you want or what you need, what good is it?

FRIAR LAURENCE. That's blasphemy! I want to see a lawyer!

PRINCE. You mean innocent until proven guilty, trial before a jury, that sort of thing?

FRIAR LAURENCE. Yes.

PRINCE. I have a simpler justice system.

(The music cuts out.)

Torture. Confession. Execution.

FRIAR LAURENCE. I don't like it.

PRINCE.

THEN YOU'RE IN TROUBLE.
THERE'S NO ATTORNEYS HERE.
I'M THE

BOTH.

ONLY LAW THAT THIS CITY KNOWS!

FRIAR LAURENCE.   I know.

PRINCE.

THERE'S NO DUE PROCESS AND MIRANDA IS THE
    SHIPWRECKED DAUGHTER OF PROSPERO.
UNDERSTAND THIS ISN'T PERSONAL
BUT I'VE GOT TWO IMPORTANT FAM'LIES IN PAIN
AND I RULE PEOPLE FOR WHOM EXECUTION
IS THE WAY THEY LIKE TO BE ENTERTAINED.

(The music cuts out.)

FRIAR LAURENCE. That's the sickest thing I've ever heard.

PRINCE.

THEN YOU'RE IN TROUBLE.
THAT STARTS WITH "T" AND
THAT RHYMES WITH "P" AND
THAT'S THE FIRST LETTER IN THE WORD
"PRIEST."

(Song ends)

So you better help yourself out here. Why would Romeo, a Montague, seek out Juliet, a Capulet, in the first place?

(With the musical transition, the lights change.)

6. EXT. A STREET IN VERONA

(A depressed **ROMEO** *enters up center and sits on the bench left.* **MERCUTIO** *tries to cheer him up like Bluto cheered up Flounder in* Animal House*.)*

ROMEO. Mercutio, let me have a torch so I can set myself on fire.

MERCUTIO. Being but heavy, you will bear the light.

ROMEO. What?

MERCUTIO. Gentle Romeo, we must have you dance. Your soul of lead stakes you to the ground so you cannot move.

ROMEO. I just want to sit down for like 5 seconds.

MERCUTIO. You are a lover. Borrow Cupid's wings, and soar with them above a common bound.

ROMEO. I just want to sit down for like 5 seconds.

*(***ROMEO*** *feeds the pigeons.)*

MERCUTIO. You are too sore enpierced with his shaft to soar with his light feathers, and so bound you cannot bound a pitch above dull woe.

ROMEO. Yeah, I guess.

*(***BENVOLIO*** *enters upstage and sizes up the situation.)*

MERCUTIO. If love be rough with you, be rough with love; prick love for pricking, and you beat love down!

BENVOLIO. Hey, there's naked girls and free booze down the street.[6]

MERCUTIO. Really? Adieu!

(He claps **ROMEO** *on the shoulder and exits down right.)*

ROMEO. Thanks, Benvolio. I can't understand him.

BENVOLIO. Me neither.

---

6 See Appendix 6 for alternate lyrics and dialogue.

ROMEO. Must I be reminded of Rosaline? "Me" was a name she called herself.

(bawls madly)

I can't believe she's gone!

(ROMEO runs off down left.)

BENVOLIO. Man, you need therapy.

(BENVOLIO follows ROMEO. CAPULET and PARIS enter up right.)

CAPULET. Thank God you have finally returned to Verona, Paris.

PARIS. I've arranged to have my vineyard transferred to you upon my marriage to Juliet.

(FRIAR LAURENCE enters down left.)

CAPULET. Good. Hi, Friar.

FRIAR LAURENCE. Can't chat.

(FRIAR LAURENCE exits down right.)

CAPULET. Wow. He's moving like someone told him there's naked girls and free booze.[7] Anyway, I want to have a "Welcome Back, Paris" party at Chateau Capulet.

PARIS. This is Italy.

CAPULET. At *Villa* Capulet. Though we just had that big bon voyage party last week –

PARIS. This is Italy.

CAPULET. – *Arrividerci* party last week. It's a two-part party, that's what it is.

PARIS. I am honored, Lord Capulet. But I think you need a better reason for the event.

CAPULET. The Fourth of July.

PARIS. Okay. Lord Capulet, this is a party to celebrate my engagement to Juliet. Why don't we just call it an engagement party?

---

7 See Appendix 6 for alternate lyrics and dialogue.

(Lights change, focusing on the doorway to **JULIET**'s *chamber.* **CAPULET** *sits facing upstage on an ornate bench stage right.)*

7. INT. JULIET'S CHAMBER – FLASH-BACK

*(***JULIET** *enters, scream-singing #3 "Juliet's Protest.")*

JULIET.

AH!
FATHER, IF YOU PROMISE ME TO PARIS,
I'LL HAVE SEX WITH SERVANTS TO EMBARRASS[8]
YOU AND MOTHER IN YOUR HIGH SOCIETY.
I WILL HAVE THE FINAL SAY WHO'S RIGHT FOR ME!
AH!

*(***JULIET** *exits, scream-singing.)*

8. EXT. THE STREET IN VERONA

(Lights restore. **CAPULET** *and* **PARIS** *as before.)*

CAPULET. Trust me, we better call it a Fourth of July party. Gregory!

*(***GREGORY** *the servant enters up right.)*

GREGORY. Yes, Lord Capulet.

CAPULET. We're having an immense party.

GREGORY. Ah, the engagement party of Juliet and Lord Paris.

*(***CAPULET** *strikes* **GREGORY**.)*

CAPULET. It's a Fourth of July party. Where's your patriotism?

GREGORY. But this is Italy.

*(***CAPULET** *retrieves a box from right.)*

---

8 See Appendix 6 for alternate lyrics and dialogue.

CAPULET. Deliver these 400 invitations in five hours.

PARIS. This Fourth of July party is starting to appeal to me.

CAPULET. We'll get red, white, and blue bunting.

PARIS. Like something out of *The Music Man.*

> *(They exit right.* **GREGORY** *weeps.* **ROMEO** *and* **BENVOLIO** *return.* **ROMEO** *hits* **GREGORY**.*)*

ROMEO. Knock it off!

GREGORY. Why do you strike me?

ROMEO. There's only one bad mood in Verona and it belongs to me.

BENVOLIO. Why do you weep? Do you fear us Montagues?

GREGORY. No, I have to tell this entire list of people about a party m'lord is throwing tonight.

BENVOLIO. You can't do that in five hours. There's 400 names on that list.

GREGORY. I am not worried about the number. I have done it before. But I can't read, so I don't know who to tell or where to go.

> *(***BENVOLIO** *takes the list.)*

BENVOLIO. Let me see that. Your master has invited the Martinos, Count Anselm and his beautiful sisters, the Widow Vitruvio, Signoir Placentio and his nieces— listen to this: the fair Rosaline.

> *(***ROMEO** *takes the list.)*

ROMEO. Sure enough, Rosaline, Livia, Valentio and his cousin Tybalt. Lucio, and the lively Helena, the Prince of Morrocco, the Prince of Arragon, Antonio—

GREGORY. The Merchant of Venice?

ROMEO. No, The Duke of Milan. Antipholus of Ephesus, Antipholus of Syracuse, Petruchio and Bianca, Katherine and Biondello—

BENVOLIO. The wife-swappers.

ROMEO. Yes. *(They share a lascivious laugh.)* Friar Laurence, Michelangelo, Titian, Raphael, Verdi, Davinci, Vermicelli, Al Dente, the Tiramisus, Antonio.

GREGORY. You said him already.

ROMEO. Antonio the Merchant of Venice.

(**BENVOLIO** *takes the list and fabricates the inclusion of the next two names.* **ROMEO** *likes the idea.*)

BENVOLIO. Romeo and Benvolio of the House of Montague, Hal and Judy Daugherty, Susan Lucci, Victoria Principal and Dr. Harry Grossman.

GREGORY. The plastic surgeon?

BENVOLIO. Yes.

GREGORY. Are you sure the list says "Romeo and Benvolio of the House of Montague"?

BENVOLIO. Well, they're on the l — oh, that's right, you can't read.

GREGORY. How do I know you didn't put Romeo and Benvolio's names on that list just to mess with me?

ROMEO. How do you know we didn't put a whole *bunch* of silly names on that list just to mess with you?

GREGORY. For some reason I trust you. Now, if you'll excuse me, I've got to deliver invitations to the Martinos, Count Anselm and his beautiful sisters, the Widow Vitruvio, Signoir Placentio and his nieces, the fair Rosaline. Livia, Valentio and his cousin Tybalt. Lucio, and the lively Helena, the Prince of Morrocco, the Prince of Arragon, Antonio, the Duke of Milan, Antipholus of Ephesus, Antipholus of Syracuse, Petruchio and Bianca, Katherine and Biondello, the wife-swappers. Friar Laurence, Michelangelo, Titian, Raphael, Verdi, Davinci, Vermicelli, Al Dente, the Tiramisus, Antonio the Merchant of Venice, Romeo and Benvolio

GREGORY. *(cont.)* of the House of Montague, Hal and Judy Daugherty, Susan Lucci, Victoria Principal and Dr. Harry Grossman, the plastic surgeon.

BENVOLIO. You have a great memory.

GREGORY. I can't read, so I better.

(*During* **GREGORY**'s *big speech,* **ROMEO** *and* **BENVOLIO** *are given invitations.* **FRIAR** *crosses through.* **GREGORY** *gives him an invite and exits.*)

FRIAR LAURENCE. What's this?

BENVOLIO. Hi, Friar.

FRIAR LAURENCE. Hello, boys.

ROMEO. This is great! I'll see Rosaline, I'll explain everything.

BENVOLIO. You'll see her in the presence of other girls and you can compare and contrast. I'm telling you she is a dog. Woof, woof.

ROMEO. I don't know, Benvolio.

(*#4, the jazz waltz "See Other People," begins.*)

BENVOLIO. Romeo, there's one sure fire solution to how you're feeling.

(*sings*)

JUST SEE OTHER PEOPLE.[9]
BY THAT I MEAN DATE.

ROMEO.

BY DATE YOU MEAN GO OUT,
YOU MEAN PROCREATE.

BENVOLIO.

I MEAN DO THE NASTY.

ROMEO.

MAKE A BEAST WITH TWO BACKS?

BENVOLIO.

NO MORE SPANKING THE MONKEY
ALONE IN THE SACK.

9 See Appendix 6 for alternate lyrics and dialogue.

ROMEO. I don't –

BENVOLIO. Yeah, you do, I can hear the bed creak.

ROMEO. What are you doing in my bedrooom!

BENVOLIO. Shh!

> *(sings again)*
> WETTING ONE'S WILLIE IS
> PART OF SURVIVAL.

ROMEO.

> YOUR MIXED METAPHORS
> ARE MERCUTIO'S RIVAL.

BENVOLIO.

> JUST SEE OTHER PEOPLE.
> YOU'RE YOUNG, RICH, AND BLESSED.
> YOU'RE A PAIN IN THE ASS!

ROMEO.

> I CALL IT DEPRESSED.

> **(ROMEO** *runs off, followed by* **BENVOLIO**. *Lights change.)*

9. INT. DUNGEON

PRINCE. The servant confirms your presence. But we don't have a complete statement from him yet.

FRIAR LAURENCE. Why not?

PRINCE. He has to learn to read and write, and that takes time.

FRIAR LAURENCE. What about Benvolio's statement?

PRINCE. Benvolio has disappeared. I think maybe you killed him, too.

FRIAR. You haven't any proof.

PRINCE. I'm the Prince. I don't need proof.

FRIAR LAURENCE. C'mon, work with me here.

PRINCE. All right. Some things just don't add up here. Like this Rosaline character. Nobody's ever seen her. And why would Capulet give the invitations to a servant who can't read? Doesn't he even know his own household?

FRIAR. That's the way it happened.

PRINCE. How would you know? Unless you were there? Yes, maybe it happened a little more like this.

(Lights change with a musical transition. See #4, measure 63.)

10. EXT. A STREET IN VERONA/| INT. THE DUNGEON

*(The **PRINCE** shoves the **FRIAR** into the street. **ROMEO** and **BENVOLIO** return. **FRIAR** has a foot in each reality. The **PRINCE** opines a version of events.)*

ROMEO. Oh, Friar Larry, I don't know what to do anymore.

FRIAR LAURENCE. I'll pray for you, Romeo.

PRINCE. Your offer of prayer was an empty measure.

FRIAR LAURENCE. Look, I just do what the Pope says we're supposed to do, all right?!

BENVOLIO. You and your God have failed us.

PRINCE. You needed a quick fix or you'd lose yet another parishioner.

*(**CAPULET** and **GREGORY** cross through.)*

CAPULET. *(To **GREGORY**.)* It's a Fourth of July party. Where's your goddamn patriotism?[10] Hi, Friar. *(**GREGORY** gives **FRIAR** an invitation.)*

FRIAR LAURENCE. Hello.

PRINCE. Capulet's party fit into your plan to manipulate

Romeo's emotions.

ROMEO. I don't know what to do, Friar Larry.

(The three of them continue #4, "See Other People".)

FRIAR LAURENCE. Well, why not

(sings)

SEE OTHER PEOPLE. GET OUT OF YOUR FUNK.

BENVOLIO.
THAT'S REALLY GREAT ADVICE FROM A
FRANCISCAN MONK

FRIAR LAURENCE.
I MEAN DO THE NASTY. I MEAN YOU GET DOWN.[11]
NO MORE MILKING THE POPE OR PUNCHING THE
CLOWN.

ROMEO & BENVOLIO.
THIS MAN OF THE CLOTH SAYS
GO AND GET SOME TODAY.

FRIAR LAURENCE.
I'VE NOT BEEN TO HELL
BUT I SURE KNOW THE WAY!

*(**FRIAR** and **BENVOLIO** start to leave.)*

ROMEO.
ROSALINE CARES NOT FOR ME.
SHE GOT HER TO A NUNNERY.
A VOW OF CHASTITY SHE'S SPOKEN.

FRIAR LAURENCE.
SHE'LL NOT ADHERE TO ABSTINENCE
I KNOW FROM MY EXPERIENCE THAT
CHASTITY'S A VOW THAT'S OFTEN BROKEN SO…

ROMEO, BENVOLIO, & FRIAR LAURENCE.[12]
SEE OTHER PEOPLE

BENVOLIO.
I MEAN SHE'S A WHORE.

FRIAR LAURENCE.
THERE'S FISH IN THE OCEAN.

11, 12 See Appendix 6 for alternate lyrics and dialogue.

BENVOLIO.

    I MEAN PUSSY GALORE.

ROMEO.

    I'LL ASK SOMEONE OUT.

    I'VE GOT CARNIVAL TICKETS.

BENVOLIO.

    OH, TEAR THOSE THINGS UP.

FRIAR LAURENCE.

    AND GO DO SOMETHING WICKED.

ROMEO & BENVOLIO.

    FOR A CELIBATE PRIEST

    YOU'VE GOT BEAU COUP KNOW HOW.

ROMEO.

    I'LL SEE OTHER PEOPLE.

FRIAR LAURENCE & BENVOLIO.

    YOU'LL SEE OTHER PEOPLE.

ROMEO.

    I'LL SEE OTHER PEOPLE

ALL THREE.

    I VOW!

    (Tableau.)

11. INT. DUNGEON

(Lights change. The **PRINCE** *stands over the* **FRIAR**.*)*

FRIAR LAURENCE. That's not what happened at all!

PRINCE. And even if Romeo caused a scene, you'd revenge yourself on Capulet.

FRIAR LAURENCE. That's doesn't even make sense. Why would I seek revenge on Capulet?

PRINCE. He didn't invite you to his party.

FRIAR LAURENCE. He did too invite me to his party. Look! Here's my invitation right here.

PRINCE. This says "Victoria Principal and Dr. Harry Grossman."

FRIAR LAURENCE. The servant was illiterate.

PRINCE. Tell me something I don't know.

FRIAR LAURENCE. I wouldn't want to see Romeo or Juliet dead. I loved those kids. I didn't know Juliet as well, but I felt some kind of cosmic bond between us.

(#5A "Transition" plays as lights change.)

12. INT. JULIET'S CHAMBER

(JULIET scampers on petulantly, trailed by the **NURSE.** *Note:* **NURSE** *is played by the actor who plays* **FRIAR LAURENCE.** *There's no time for a costume change, but the two characters are distinguishable visually. The* **FRIAR** *always has the wooden cross around his neck. The* **NURSE** *always holds a lacy handkercheif.)*

JULIET. Noooooogetawayfromme!

NURSE. Juliet, you must allow me to brush your hair!

JULIET. I said, "No!" Nurse, I don't want you to touch my hair. I don't want anyone touching my hair. I want it to get ratty and matted and fall out so I have to wear a wig like yours. I don't want anyone touching my hair. I don't want to be beautiful. I want to be ugly.

NURSE. You can tell this is a wig?

JULIET. Yes, I can tell it's a wig. Now get out.

(JULIET sits down and looks through a newspaper.)

NURSE. What are you doing with that newspaper?

JULIET. I'm going to get a job. I hear Duke Senior over at Forest of Arden needs girls to dress up like boys.

NURSE. I hear he wants boys to dress up like girls to dress up like boys.

(**JULIET** *flops down on the bench on her back.*)[13]

JULIET. I hate everything.

NURSE. (*Chuckling*) My late husband was right!

JULIET. What are you laughing about?

NURSE. When you were a little girl, you bumped your head and fell on your face. My late husband Jerry said, "When she gets a little older, she'll be falling on her back." And it's true, you did, just now.

JULIET. Yeah. He was hilarious, Nurse. The funniest pervert ever!

NURSE. You can really tell this is a wig?

JULIET. Yes, I can tell it's a wig. Now get out.

NURSE. Juliet, what's wrong with you?

JULIET. I don't want to marry Paris.

NURSE. Juliet, you mustn't say such things.

(**LADY CAPULET** *enters.*)

Lady Capulet, Juliet says she doesn't want to marry Paris.

LADY CAPULET. Oh, I know, sweetheart, you're frightened. You're just a little girl.

(*The* **NURSE** *chuckles at a fond memory.*)

What's so funny?

NURSE. I can't help but recall my late husband Jerry saying, "Thank heaven for little girls because they don't mind running around naked."

LADY CAPULET. Why don't you want to marry Paris?

JULIET. He's a man of wax.

LADY CAPULET. You mean he's like a tall, slender, fragrant candle.

NURSE. You mean he melts when he kisses your fiery lips.

---

13 See Appendix 6 for alternate lyrics and dialogue.

JULIET. I mean he's not a real man. He's like a wax figure. Beautiful but weak…He's gross, Mother. I'm going to get a job.

LADY CAPULET. Doing what? Selling yourself?

JULIET. If I have to!

NURSE. You know, that reminds me of how Jerry and I met.

JULIET and LADY CAPULET. Shut up.

JULIET. Mother, I don't love him.

> (**LADY CAPULET**, **NURSE**, *and* **JULIET** *sing #5B, "True Love to Me."*)

LADY CAPULET. Juliet, that doesn't matter.

> *(sings)*

> I GOT MARRIED TO YOUR DAD TO
> ALLY OUR FAMILIES.
> HE GOT BORED WHEN YOU WERE BORN BUT I GOT
>   THIS HOUSE.
> HE'S MARRIED TO HIS WORK
> THOUGH I'M NOT SURE WHAT THAT IS.
> IT'S IN NAME ONLY, GIRL, THAT I'M HIS SPOUSE.
> *(chorus)*
> BUT HOW I LOVE HIM.
> HE'S STILL MY EVERYTHING
> THOUGH HE'S FLATULENT AND OFTEN VISITS WHORES.
> OH, HOW I LOVE HIM.
> I KNOW HE TRULY CARES FOR ME
> THOUGH I'M DEPRIVED OF SLEEP BECAUSE HE SNORES.

NURSE.

> I GOT MARRIED 'CAUSE WE HAD TO
> AND HE WAS A DRUNKEN LOUT.
> I LOST THE KID 'CAUSE HE HAD A REAL MEAN STREAK.
> WHEN HE DIED HE WAS BROKE,
> LEAVING ME A LOAD OF DEBT.
> THERE WERE NO BENEFITS OF WHICH TO SPEAK.

> *(chorus)*

NURSE.

BUT HOW I MISS HIM.

HE'S STILL MY EVERYTHING.

I MISS HIS DIRTY JOKES AND CREEPY TOUCH.

OH, YES, I MISS HIM, AND HOW HE CARED FOR ME,

EVEN THOUGH HE NEVER CARED THAT MUCH.

(Speaking in rhythm, **NURSE** *and* **LADY CAPULET** *assault* **JULIET** *with advice.)*

LADY CAPULET.

DON'T BRING THE FAM'LY NAME DISGRACE.

THINGS LIKE THIS ARE COMMONPLACE.

NURSE.

HIS HABITS WILL BECOME BEGUILING

EVEN IF HE'S PEDOPHILING.[14]

LADY CAPULET.

SEX, YOU'RE RIGHT, IT WON'T BE FUN

BUT ONE MALE HEIR AND THEN IT'S DONE.

"STAND BY YOUR MAN" IS ETIQUETTE.

SO SAITH GOOD OL' QUEEN WYNETTE.

NURSE.

BUT THERE'S NO REASON TO BE NICE.

LADY CAPULET.

IT'S MARRIAGE, DEAR, NOT PARADISE.

JULIET.

NO MORE ADVICE!

THANK YOU ALL FOR TRYING BUT

I'M DIFFERENT THAN YOU HAGS.

I'VE GOT TITS AND ASS[15]

NURSE.

AND HAIR

JULIET.

AND MY OWN VOICE.

I DON'T KNOW WHERE YOU'RE ENSCONCED

BUT I LIVE IN THE RENAISSANCE

I'M ENLIGHTENED AND I'M MAKING MY OWN CHOICE.

14, 15 See Appendix 6 for alternate lyrics and dialogue.

(Upstage, **PARIS** *crosses through in SLOW MOTION.)*

AND HOW I HATE HIM!
I DETEST THE WAY HE SMELLS.
HIS COLOGNE IS CHOKING ALL OF ITALY.
OH, HOW I HATE HIM.

(PARIS *appears in another opening upstage left. This time he's carrying a balloon on a stick.)*

WHEN ALL IS DONE AND SAID,
I'D RATHER WIND UP DEAD
THAN GRANT HIM MY MAIDENHEAD.

LADY CAPULET.
THAT SOUNDS LIKE LOVE TO ME.

NURSE.
IT SURELY DOES.

JULIET.
OH, GOD ABOVE, IT CAN'T BE

ALL.
                              TRUE LOVE TO ME.

(Lights go to blue.)

13. EXT. THE STREET IN VERONA

(Lights up. **ROMEO** *and* **BENVOLIO** *enter down left.* **ROMEO** *has the invitation.)*

ROMEO. What if someone recognizes us at the Capulet party?

(MERCUTIO *enters down right.* **ROMEO** *hides the invitation.)*

MERCUTIO. Hey, guys, are you going to the Capulet party?

ROMEO. Don't be ridiculous. How would we get an invitation?

MERCUTIO. *(holding an invitation)* Tell an illiterate servant your name is Susan Lucci.

BENVOLIO. Well, we're going to the church carnival.

ROMEO. At the church on the other side of town. Why don't you meet us there?

MERCUTIO. You guys are so immature. Go to a dumb church carnival when you can go to a big ball at the Capulets. But maybe they have the baptismal clown dunking booth.

BENVOLIO. Yeah, that's why we're going to the carnival.

MERCUTIO. Where are your carnival tickets?

ROMEO. Oh, well –

MERCUTIO. That carnival's too wild for you guys. But you're in luck. Because you guys are coming with me.

*(**MERCUTIO** sings #6 "It's a Pity You're Not Me.")*

BECAUSE IT'S WELL KNOWN I AM CHARMING.
I KNOW THAT I'M VERY STRONG.
MY RAPIER WIT IS DISARMING
AND I'VE GOT A DICK LIKE KING KONG.[16]
I'M SURE YOU'VE DISCERNED
I'VE GOT MONEY TO BURN,
I'M AS PERFECT AS ONE GUY CAN BE,

(chorus)

I'M WITTY, I'M PRETTY, I'M PRINCE OF THE CITY
AND IT'S JUST A PITY..YOU'RE NOT ME!
(verse)

I DRINK, BUT I'M NEVER HUNG OVER.
I PLOW THROUGH THE LADIES THREE DEEP.[17]
I WAKE UP SMELLING LIKE CLOVER.
THAT IS IF I'VE BOTHERED TO SLEEP.
IF YOU ORBIT MY WORLD,
YOU'LL GET SECOND HAND GIRLS.
I'M GOD'S GIFT TO WOMEN, YOU SEE.

16, 17 See Appendix 6 for alternate lyrics and dialogue.

(chorus)

I'M WITTY, I'M PRETTY, I'M GAY (AS IN GIDDY),
AND IT'S JUST A PITY...YOU'RE NOT ME.

*(During the bridge, **MERCUTIO** sits right with one arm around **ROMEO** and one around **BENVOLIO**. They have a meeting under his chin. **MERCUTIO** is so self-absorbed he doesn't hear them.)*

I SEE THAT QUEEN MAB HAS BEEN WITH YOU.
SHE IS THE FAIRIES' MIDWIFE.

ROMEO.   Oh, geez.

LET'S GET AWAY FROM THIS YAHOO.
HIS WIT CUTS LIKE AN OLD RUSTY KNIFE.

MERCUTIO.

HER CHARIOT'S AN EMPTY HAZEL-NUT
MADE BY THE JOINER SQUIRREL OR OLD GRUB.

BENVOLIO.

I THINK MAB TRANSLATES TO "SLATTERN" OR "SLUT".

ROMEO.

HE SOUNDS LIKE SOME DRUNK IN A PUB.

MERCUTIO.

AND THEN DREAMS HE OF CUTTING FOREIGN
     THROATS,
OF BREACHES, AMBUSCADOES, SPANISH BLADES.

ROMEO & BENVOLIO.

MERCUTIO, GO TAKE A JUMP IN THE MOAT!
WE GOT ONLY THROUGH THE EIGHTH GRADE.

MERCUTIO.

(verse)

Ha ha!
THE TWO OF YOU ARE JUST JEALOUS
OF MY WIT AND CHARM AND PANACHE.

ROMEO AND BENVOLIO.

NO, YOU JUST DON'T LISTEN.

MERCUTIO.
> That's right!
> WE'VE GOT A PARTY TO CRASH.
> MY GENIUS IS WOND'ROUS,
> MY SINGING IS THUND'ROUS,
> THE SUNRISE WAS DESIGNED FOR ME.
> I INVENTED THE WHEEL,
> I CAN GET YOU A DEAL
> ON A LOW MILEAGE CARRIAGE,
> OH, IT'S SUCH A STEAL!
> I'VE GOT DREAMS AND GOALS
> TO RIP OFF BILLY JOEL.

ROMEO AND BENVOLIO. *(sampling "Pianoman")*
> YES, THERE'S SOME PLACE THAT WE'D RATHER BE.

MERCUTIO.
> OH, WHAT A PITY YOU'RE NOT ME!

(Mercutio has an arm around each of his "buddies" as they all exit. The lights change and...)

14. INT. DUNGEON

(...The **PRINCE** *regales the* **FRIAR** *with the harmonica solo from "Pianoman.")*

PRINCE. If you're gonna be in prison, you oughta learn to play one of these.

FRIAR LAURENCE. If you want to pin the rap on someone, try Mercutio. That guy was a loose cannon. He thought he was so funny, but he talked so weird.

PRINCE. "O then I see Queen Mab hath been with you. She is the fairies' midwife, and she comes in shape no bigger than an agot-stone on the forefinger of an alderman, drawn with a team of little atomi over men's noses as they lie asleep." You mean weird like that?

FRIAR LAURENCE. Yeah.

PRINCE. What's weird about it?

FRIAR LAURENCE. Nothing.

PRINCE. I'm glad we agree. I'd like to blame Mercutio, but I can't. There are witnesses who saw him at the carnival.

(*Lights change.*)

15. EXT. THE ROAD OUTSIDE VILLA CAPULET

(*In #7,* **ROMEO** *and* **BENVOLIO** *establish the "Fantastic Mask" fanfare. Whenever anyone puts on a mask, the pianist plays a short gliss down. Whenever anyone takes off a mask, the pianist plays a short gliss up. See #36.*)

BENVOLIO. Hey, put these masks on.

ROMEO. Wow! This is a

(*sings*)

FANTASTIC MASK!

(*They take off the masks.*)

BENVOLIO. Thanks. I got them at the apothecary. No one will ever recognize us.

MERCUTIO. (*offstage*) Hey! Romeo. Benvolio.

ROMEO. Shit.[18]

MERCUTIO. Where'd ya go?

(**ROMEO** *and* **BENVOLIO** *put on the masks.* **MERCUTIO** *enters.*)

Excuse me, citizens, have you seen my friends Romeo and Benvolio?

ROMEO. Yes, they were headed to the carnival.

MERCUTIO. Thanks. I better catch up. They're lost without me.

---

18 See Appendix 6 for alternate lyrics and dialogue.

(**MERCUTIO** *exits. They take off the masks.*)

ROMEO. These things are worth everything you paid and more!

ROMEO & BENVOLIO. *(singing)*

FANTASTIC MASK!

(A bouncy Gilbert & Sullivan-like rhythm takes them off and...)

16. INT. HALL AT VILLA CAPULET

(...and brings on the **CAPULETS, PARIS, FRIAR LAURENCE,** *and* **TYBALT,** *who enter "sailor-skipping" and singing #7, "Hello, Drink Up, Chow Down.")*

*(***LORD CAPULET** *wears an Uncle Sam top hat, a red sash reading "Happy Fourth of July." He brandishes a scepter or drum major's baton. Everyone else forms a chorus near the bench left.)*

(Note: in this scene, the actor playing **MERCUTIO** *joins the chorus as* **ANTIPHOLUS.** *Shortly, the actors playing* **ROMEO, BENVOLIO,** *and* **JULIET** *will appear as other party-goers, making 9 actors seem like 30. See Appendix 2.)*

CAPULET.

HELLO.

CHORUS.

HELLO.

CAPULET.

WELCOME

CHORUS.

THANK YOU.

CAPULET.

TO MY FOURTH OF JULY PARTY. DRINK UP.

CHORUS.

DRINK UP.

CAPULET.

CHOW DOWN.

CHORUS.

CHOW DOWN.

CAPULET.

JOIN THE CELEBRATION TO HAIL

CHORUS.

WE HAIL

CAPULET.

THE DAY

CHORUS.

THE DAY THAT NOBLE PARIS CAME HOME.

CAPULET.

NOT SO.

CHORUS.

NOT SO?

CAPULET.

TODAY

CHORUS.

TODAY

CAPULET.

IS THE BIRTHDAY OF OUR NATION.

CHORUS.

OKAY, WHATE'ER, YOU SAY.

HOW ABOUT THOSE FOUNDING FATHERS?

(The **CHORUS** *produces Independence Day accessories and puts them on.)*

CAPULET.

DRINK UP.

CHORUS.

DRINK UP.

CAPULET.

CHOW DOWN.

CHORUS.

CHOW DOWN.

CAPULET & CHORUS.

JOIN THE PATRIOTIC THRONG.

(The **CHORUS** *dryly oohs and ahhs at the celebrated attendees, who cross through up center or are pointed out by* **CAPULET** *in the audience.)*

CAPULET. *(pointing upstage)*

HERE IS ANSELM, THE GOOD COUNT,

CHORUS.

OOH!

CAPULET. *(pointing upstage)*

AND BOTH HIS LOVELY SISTERS,

CHORUS.

AH!

CAPULET. *(pointing to audience.)*

KATHERINE THE SHREW,

AND HER BEAU PETRUCHIO!

CHORUS.

WOW!

CAPULET.

LOOK THERE!

CHORUS. *(wrong way)*

LOOK WHERE?

CAPULET. *(corrects them)*

RIGHT THERE.

CHORUS. *(right way)*

OH, THERE.

CAPULET.

IT IS MICHAELANGELO.

CHORUS.

DRESSED UP LIKE ABRAHAM LINCOLN,

IT'S MICHAELANGELO!

(MICHAELANGELO/LINCOLN appears for a second, saying "Four score and seven years ago..." PARIS exits. CHORUS does a spit take as JULIET screams on her way in.)

JULIET.

AH!

CAPULET.

HONEY, WHEN YOU SCREAM LIKE THAT YOU SCARE US.

JULIET.

FATHER, YOU FORGET I CAN'T STAND PARIS.
YOU CANNOT ARRANGE MY FAUX ENGAGEMENT
WITHOUT SPARKING FIRE OF MY ENRAGEMENT.

(The Revolutionary War flag with 13 stars, deftly handled by MAN 1 and WOMAN 3, appears upstage.)

CAPULET.

YOU SEE THAT FLAG MY PRETTY LITTLE INGENUE.
OUR COUNTRY'S STARS AND STRIPES ARE NOT
ABOUT YOU... *(The flag disappears.)* SO DRINK UP.

CHORUS.

DRINK UP.

CAPULET.

CHOW DOWN.

CHORUS.

CHOW DOWN.

CAPULET.

WE HOLD THESE TRUTHS SELF-EVIDENT.

CHORUS.

JUST AS SURE AS SHIT THAT
WASHINGTON WAS OUR FIRST PRESIDENT.

(All skip around the bench, disguising the exit of ANTIPHOLUS and the entrance of the PRINCE. The CHORUS kneels, effectively disappearing as the lights change.)

17. INT. DUNGEON

PRINCE. Yes, that's all here in the record. But how did Romeo and Benvolio get into the party?

FRIAR LAURENCE. Each of them had a

(he sings)

FANTASTIC MASK!

PRINCE. Yeah, yeah, yeah.

(puts on a mask)

Who am I?

FRIAR LAURENCE. You're Prince Escalus.

PRINCE. That's right, and this the most...

(sings)

FANTASTIC MASK

(speaks)

...money can buy. *(removes mask)* There must have been some other reason those two could get in.

(Lights change.)

18. EXT. VILLA CAPULET

*(**BARNEY FIFE,** an officer of the law, prevents **ROMEO** and **BENVOLIO** from entering. Note: In some productions, the **GATEKEEPER** from* The Wizard of Oz *has had all of Barney's scenes. See Appendix 1.)*

BARNEY. Hang on there, Fella. Deputy Sheriff Barney Fife. Just where do you think you're going?

ROMEO. Say that again.

BARNEY. Where do you think you're going?

ROMEO. I think he'd be perfect.

BARNEY. What are you talking about? How come you're wearing masks? Just whattaya you trying to pull, mister?

BENVOLIO. Yes, he's perfect.

ROMEO. Forgive us. My friend and I are casting a new play and we couldn't help notice your latent acting ability.

BARNEY. Really. Well, I was in drama club in high school. You learn *a lot* about acting from being a stagehand.

ROMEO. You are too modest. The play is *Much Ado About Nothing* and you're perfect for the role of Constable Dogberry.

BENVOLIO. And certainly we'd want your technical advice on law enforcement.

ROMEO. You'll have to go on a publicity tour, be seen with starlets, that sort of thing.

BARNEY. Well, I do fancy the ladies.

ROMEO. You and me both, my friend. Now, we've got to cast some other parts and we need to scope out the tail. *(BENVOLIO hits ROMEO)* I mean research the talent pool.

BARNEY. Oh, sure, sure, sure, sure. You know some of these girls have been dipped in pretty sauce. Now move along.

(The lights change as they go inside...)

19. INT. HALL AT VILLA CAPULET

(...where the happy guests resume #7 and the skipping dance.)

FRIAR LAURENCE. Hello, Lord Capulet. Where's young Paris, your future son-in-law?

(CAPULET and the CHORUS sing. ANTIPHOLUS returns.)

CAPULET.

SHUT UP!

CHORUS.

SHUT UP!

CAPULET.

PIPE DOWN.

CHORUS.

PIPE DOWN.

CAPULET.

THAT'S NOT FOR JULIET TO KNOW. WE HAIL

CHORUS.

WE HAIL

CAPULET.

THIS DAY

CHORUS.

THIS DAY,

(ROMEO, JULIET, and BENVOLIO pop on and off in the 3 upstage entryways.)

ALL.

THIS DAY OF INDEPENDENCE.

CAPULET. *(to FRIAR)*

SO CATCH MY DRIFT AND SEAL YOUR LIPS.

CHORUS.

YOU'RE OUT OF GOOD MERLOT.

CAPULET.   My bad.

HERE IS CORDELIA

(Other guests appear upstage or in the audience.)

CHORUS.

OOH!

CAPULET.

AND BOTH HER HEINOUS SISTERS,

CHORUS.

AH!

CAPULET.

ANTIPHOLUS, AND VICTOR TIRAMISU.

VICTOR. *(aka Cosby)* There's pudding in the cake!

CAPULET. Look there!

> (**ROMEO** *and* **BENVOLIO** *bound through like magnificent gazelles. The* **CHORUS** *looks the wrong way.*)

CHORUS.

AVAST!

CAPULET. *(corrects them)*

THOSE TWO!

CHORUS.

IN MASKS!

CAPULET.

THEY COULD BE MONTAGUES.

CHORUS.

TWO GUYS DRESSED UP IN MASKS SO GREAT
THEY COULD BE MONTAGUES.

> (**CHORUS** *kneels, lights change.*)

20. INT. DUNGEON

FRIAR LAURENCE. So I didn't think the masks were that big of a thing. I thought it was odd to have a Fourth of July party.

PRINCE. What's wrong with a Fourth of July party? What are you, some kinda Bolshevik?

FRIAR LAURENCE. No. What's a Bolshevik?

PRINCE. Someone who'd like to see our way of life destroyed.

FRIAR LAURENCE. Oh, no, I like our way of life. I'm a monarchist.

PRINCE. Really?

FRIAR LAURENCE. Yes, really. You are my monarch.

PRINCE. Well, wouldn't our founding fathers like to hear that shit?

(Lights broaden again.)

21. INT. HALL AT VILLA CAPULET

(TYBALT enters. The happy skipping music now sounds dangerous as TYBALT crosses to center. FRIAR LAURENCE chats with LADY CAPULET. ROMEO makes himself at home with the guests stage left.)

TYBALT. Lord Capulet.

CAPULET. Yes, Tybalt.

TYBALT. That's Romeo Montague.

CAPULET. How can you be sure? That's a

(sings)

FANTASTIC MASK!

TYBALT. Let me dispatch him to the devil now. My sword is honed for such a task.

CAPULET. Yes, but…

(TYBALT sings #8, "I Want to Kill Him.")

TYBALT.

I WANT TO KILL HIM. PLEASE LET ME KILL HIM.
I'LL CHEAT FATE AND RENEW MY SELF ESTEEM.

CAPULET.

NO, I FORBID IT. THINK OF MY PARTY.
MY SOCIAL STANDING.
WE MUST NOT CAUSE A SCENE.

TYBALT.

BUT IT'S MY DUTY TO OUR CLAN
TO TEAR HIS HEART OUT WITH MY HAND.
LOOK, OLD MAN, I'M FIG'RATIVELY DOWN ON MY
    KNEES.
JUST LET ME KILL HIM…PRETTY PLEASE.

(Bridge. **FRIAR LAURENCE** *waltzes by with* **LADY CAPULET**.*)*

I MUST ADMIT THIS IS A FEELING THAT WON'T QUIT
IF HE SURVIVES I'M LYING TO MYSELF.

FRIAR LAURENCE.

WHAT'S WITH HIM?

CAPULET.

OH WELL, YOU KNOW, HE DIDN'T EAT,
HIS SUGAR'S LOW.

(to **TYBALT***)*

HAVE A DRINK, RELAX, JESUS, YOU NEED HELP.

*(***ROMEO** *gets a drink downstage.* **TYBALT** *is close enough to strike, but* **ROMEO** *cannot hear him.)*

TYBALT.

I WANT TO SLAY HIM,
SLICE, DICE, AND FILET HIM,
MAKE THE WORLD FORGET HE HAD A PRETTY FACE.

CAPULET.

YOUR RAGE IS LUDICROUS
LIKE TITUS ANDRONICUS.

TYBALT.

YES, AND A SEVERED HEAD WOULD LIVEN UP THIS
    PLACE.
IT'S PART OF GOD'S GRAND PLAN
THAT I PROVE I'M A MAN
IN A MANNER THAT'S UNIQUELY VERONESE.
JUST LET ME KILL HIM….PRETTY PLEASE.

(Button. **LADY CAPULET** *exits.* **CHORUS** *kneels. Lights change.)*

22. INT. DUNGEON[19]

PRINCE. So now you took it upon yourself to introduce Romeo and Juliet...to foment disaster.

FRIAR LAURENCE. Oh, come on, Prince. You know that didn't happen. I did not introduce Romeo and Juliet. I wasn't even in the room when they met.

PRINCE. All right, where were you?

(The orchestra plays #9, "Porn Underscore".)

23. INT. ANTECHAMBER AT VILLA CAPULET

*(Upstage center, a desperate, adulterous embrace between **FRIAR LAURENCE** and his lusty, beautiful **PARAMOUR** is obscured by red whorehouse lighting and the garish porno theme. See also Appendix 2.)*

PARAMOUR. Make me confess, Friar!

FRIAR LAURENCE. How long has it been?

PARAMOUR. Too long!

(They make more "wild sex" noise before we cut back.)

24. INT. DUNGEON

*(When **FRIAR** lands center, music cuts out.)*

FRIAR LAURENCE. Okay, I'm not proud of that. But that's where I was.

PRINCE. Yes, she confirms that.

FRIAR LAURENCE. Really? Did she say anything?

PRINCE. How did Romeo and Juliet meet then?

(Lights change.)

---

19 See Appendix 6 for alternate lyrics and dialogue.

25. INT. HALL AT VILLA CAPULET

*(The cast ad libs party chatter for 8 beats. **LADY CAPULET** returns. Everyone freezes when **ROMEO** and **JULIET** spot one another across the room. They run to each other.)*

ROMEO. If I profane with my unworthiest hand this holy shrine, the gentle sin is this, my lips, two blushing pilgrims –

*(**JULIET** lays a most audacious kiss on him.)*

Wowzer.

*(**ROMEO** and **JULIET** freeze, too. Lights change.)*

26. INT. DUNGEON

*(All remain frozen as the **FRIAR** and the **PRINCE** talk.)*

FRIAR LAURENCE. No, no, it wasn't like that.

PRINCE. Yes, I know enough about physics to know that people just don't freeze.

FRIAR LAURENCE. The meeting of Romeo and Juliet was far more ordinary.

(All reanimate as lights change.)

27. INT. HALL AT VILLA CAPULET

*(A bossa nova begins. **ROMEO** meets a **SERVING WENCH**, who is played by the same actress that plays **BENVOLIO**. Upstage, the **CAPULETS** bicker, **ANTIPHOLUS** departs. **TYBALT** paws **JULIET** and **FRIAR LAURENCE** departs.)*

ROMEO. Excuse me, Serving Wench.

SERVING WENCH. We're out of the merlot.[20]

ROMEO. Thank you, but that isn't my question.

SERVING WENCH. Okay, okay, but let me wash the last guy out of my mouth, okay?

ROMEO. No, no…what lady's that which doth enrich the hand of yonder knight?

SERVING WENCH. I don't know. But I hear she's easy.

(ROMEO and **JULIET** *toss their drinks away and sing #10, "Use Each Other Tonight."* **PARIS** *returns and dances with the* **SERVING WENCH.** *The* **CAPU-LET***s dance lustfully. The actors who play* **FRIAR** *and* **TYBALT** *are now* **MUSICIANS** *near the piano and play rhythm instruments.)*

ROMEO.

THE FIRST TIME THAT YOU WALKED INTO THIS
ROOM YOU DIDN'T SEE ME 'CAUSE I…HADN'T
ARRIVED.
THE NEXT TIME THAT YOU ENTERED I WAS
THROWING UP OUTSIDE BECAUSE I'D…
OVER–IMBIBED.
SO MAYBE BY THE FOURTH TIME IT'LL BE FIN'LY BE
LOVE AT FIRST SI-IGHT, SO

ROMEO & JULIET.

WHY DON'T WE USE EACH OTHER TONIGHT?

JULIET.

THE FIRST TIME THAT I WALKED INTO THIS ROOM
WE HAD JUST MOVED HERE AND I…WAS EIGHT OR
NINE.
IT SEEMS SINCE THEN THAT I HAVE BEEN
SURROUNDED BY THE REEKING BREATH OF…
DRUNKEN SWINE.
I WOULD LIKE TO GET BACK AT MY FAMILY
IF FOR NO OTHER REASON THAN SPI-ITE SO

ROMEO & JULIET.

WHY DON'T WE USE EACH OTHER TONIGHT.?

---

20 See Appendix 6 for alternate lyrics and dialogue.

(**BARNEY** *crosses through, keeping an eye on things and enjoying the music.*)

ROMEO.

I'LL GENTLY HOLD YOUR HAND AND DO...LOVEY
DOVEY STUFF.

JULIET.

MY GOODNESS, YOU'RE SO HANDSOME, WELL, OKAY,
YOU'RE HANDSOME ENOUGH.

ROMEO.

THE FIRST KISS YOU HAVE GIVEN ME, IT BORDERS ON
THE HEAVENLY. MY HEARTACHE SUBSIDES.

JULIET.

HOLD ME CLOSE SO THAT MY FATHER GOES
BALLISTIC. HE WILL BE SO...HORRIFIED.

ROMEO & JULIET.

I'M ACTING OUT A PLAY I WROTE.
I'M THE STAR,
YOU'RE THE SATELLI – ITE SO
WE AGREE TO USE EACH OTHER TONIGHT.
THIS IS CALLED A *QUID PRO QUO —*
SYNCHRONICITY.

JULIET.

I'LL SCRATCH YOUR BACK[21]

ROMEO.

WHILE YOU'RE ON YOURS.

BOTH.

THAT SOUNDS GOOD TO ME.

(*She takes off his mask. Music continues under. He kisses her.*)

JULIET. You might want to buy a book on kissing. Wait a minute. You're Romeo Montague.

ROMEO. (*finger on her lips*) Shh!

JULIET. That's a fantastic mask. (*She replaces the mask.*)

ROMEO. Thanks, listen, don't tell the Capulets I'm here. They hate us.

---

21 See Appendix 6 for alternate lyrics and dialogue.

JULIET. I'm Juliet Capulet.

(Music out/Spotlight. Take. Music in/Spot out.)

ROMEO.

EVERYTHING'S EXTRANEOUS 'CAUSE I FEEL
   SIMULTANEOUS...TRUE LOVE AND HATE.
CALL ME CRAZY AND ELITE-IST BUT IT'S HER
FRUIT THAT'S THE SWEETEST
THERE'S SO MUCH AT STAKE.

JULIET. *(Singing contrapuntally)*

WHAT GOOD FORTUNE HAS BESTOWED UPON ME.
THIS BIG JAMOCHE IS GROWING ON ME.

ROMEO & JULIET.

I CAN'T STAND YOUR FAMILY SO A ONE NIGHT
STAND IS GRAND FOR ME
SO LET'S CONSPIRE TO USE EACH OTHER TONIGHT.

CHORUS.

TONIGHT, TONIGHT,

ROMEO & JULIET.

TONIGHT.

CHORUS.

WON'T BE JUST ANY NIGHT.

(Tableau.)

28. INT. HALL AT VILLA CAPULET

(Lights change. The "Hello" melody is reused for "So Far," #11. The Chorus – **ROMEO, FRIAR, SERVING WENCH, PARIS, LADY CAPULET,** *and* **TYBALT** *– converge around the bench left.* **LORD CAPULET** *is center.* **JULIET** *is right.)*

CAPULET.

SO FAR.

CHORUS.

DRINK UP.

CAPULET.

SO GOOD.

CHORUS.

CHOW DOWN.

CAPULET.

REMEMBER WHY YOU CAME HERE. TO HAIL

CHORUS.

WE HAIL

CAPULET.

THIS DAY

CHORUS.

THIS DAY THAT NOBLE PARIS CAME HOME.

JULIET. *(long note)*

WHAAAAAAT?

CHORUS.

WE DID NOT MEAN

TO SPILL THE BEANS

BUT WE DRANK WINE ON TOP OF BEER.

CAPULET.

GODDAMN, YOU STUPID FOOLS,

SHE'S NOT TO KNOW THAT.

I GAVE YOU A BAG

BUT YOU LET LOOSE THE CAT.

(LIVE SFX: A cat's meow is simulated by **MAN 2** *offstage.)*

CHORUS.

DRINK UP.

CAPULET.

GET OUT!

CHORUS.

OKAY.

CAPULET.

GET OUT!

CHORUS.

GUESS THE PARTY'S OVER.

(Fugue. **ALL** *skip and converge around* **CAPULET** *center. The* **SERVING WENCH** *scoots out.)*

CAPULET.

LOOK WHAT YOU'VE DONE NOW!

JULIET.

FATHER DON'T FORGET I CAN'T STAND PARIS!

CHORUS.

DRINK UP.

CAPULET.

GET OUT!

CHORUS.

OKAY.

CAPULET.

GET OUT!

CHORUS.

GUESS THE PARTY'S OVER.

CAPULET.

LOOK WHAT YOU'VE DONE NOW!

JULIET.

FATHER, DON'T FORGET I CAN'T STAND PARIS!

TENORS.

BELLS ARE RINGING. BELLS ARE RINGING.

CAPULET. Get out!

(**ALL** *"sailor skip" away.*)

And no looking at the fireworks!

(*Lights change, scored by the continuation of #11, "Mercutio Transition."*)

29. EXT. THE ROAD OUTSIDE VILLA CAPULET – LATER

(**MERCUTIO** *enters with his arm locked around* **BENVOLIO**'s *neck.*)

MERCUTIO. When I didn't see you guys at the carnival, I figured out you must be here.

BENVOLIO. Yeah, you must have misheard us.

MERCUTIO. Yeah, 'cause you wouldn't lie to me.

BENVOLIO. No, we wouldn't lie to you.

MERCUTIO. Hey…look what I won.

(He shows off a small stuffed animal. **ROMEO** *enters, deep in thought.)*

Romeo! Humors! Madman! Passion! Lover!
Appear thou in the likeness of a sigh!

ROMEO. Yeah, I guess.

MERCUTIO. On the day I get married, I can't decide which one of you will be my best man.

BENVOLIO. It can be Romeo. I'm busy that day.

MERCUTIO. What do you guys want to do now? I blew all my money at the baptismal clown dunking booth.

ROMEO. Well, see. I just met this girl and…

MERCUTIO. Yes, I conjure thee by Rosaline's bright eyes, by her high forehead and her scarlet lip –

ROMEO. I don't mean Rosaline. It's a different girl.

MERCUTIO. Great! She'll get me a friend and she'll get Benvolio a friend…

ROMEO. Well…

MERCUTIO. …or whatever, man! Hey – if you want me to have sex with her so you know what to do, I will. I will do that for you, man.

ROMEO. Thank you for the offer, really, but…well, it's Benvolio…he's kinda cramping my style.

MERCUTIO. Oh.

*(***ROMEO*** *mouths "I'm so sorry.")*

BENVOLIO. Oh, don't even.

ROMEO. So if you could —

MERCUTIO. Say no more.

(He puts **BENVOLIO** *in a headlock and drags him off.* **BENVOLIO** *gives* **ROMEO** *the finger.)*

MERCUTIO. *(cont.)* O, Romeo, that she were, O that she were an open arse, thou a pop'rin pear!

BENVOLIO. I hope you get a disease!

(As the last measures of #11 play, the scene transforms.)

30. EXT. ORCHARD AKA THE BALCONY SCENE

(ROMEO kneels left.)

ROMEO. But soft, what light…

(JULIET enters.)

…wow, there's Juliet.

(She sings #12, "O Romeo.")

JULIET.

O, ROMEO, ROMEO WHEREFORE ART THOU ROMEO? DENY THEY FATHER AND REFUSE THY NAME.

ROMEO. Hi! I 'm down here.

JULIET.

O, BE SOME OTHER NAME! WHAT'S IN A NAME? THAT WHICH –

(NURSE enters. Note: the following italicized dialogue ought to be changed as current events dictate.)[22]

NURSE. Juliet, only *former senate candidate Jack Ryan* would dance with me at the party. I think I can do better than *former senate candidate Jack Ryan*.

JULIET. I think you should sell when you can, you are not for all markets.

NURSE. *Just wait 'til you get old.*

(NURSE cries and runs out. JULIET resumes her cadenza.)

---

[22] See Appendix 6 for alternate lyrics and dialogue.

JULIET.

THAT WHICH WE CALL A ROSE –

(BARNEY enters, doing a signature karate chop.)

BARNEY. Thought I heard a noise.

JULIET. I'm singing.

BARNEY. You're out past the legal curfew.

JULIET. This is my balcony.

BARNEY. Every night is New Year's Eve to you darn kids!

(He exits. She strikes a poses, continuing the cadenza.)

JULIET.

A RO-O-O-O-O-SE!

ROMEO. Juliet?

JULIET. Oh, forget it.

ROMEO. Look, I really like you, but....

(He sings #13, "Why Wherefore Art Thou.")

WHY SAY "WHEREFORE" INSTEAD OF "WHY"?
BE SIMPLE AND STRAIGHT FORWARD.

JULIET.

YOU'RE MONOSYLLABIC.

ROMEO.

YEAH, SO WHAT?

JULIET.

AND YOU ARE IDIOTIC.

ROMEO.

WHY SAY "WHEREFORE" INSTEAD OF "WHY"?
WHY SAY "PARTING" INSTEAD OF "GOODBYE"?
BECAUSE "SORRY"

JULIET.

...IS PEDESTRIAN.
"SWEET SORROW" IS POETIC
AND YOUR VOCABULARY IS
PALTRY AND PATHETIC.

ROMEO.
> WHY "WHEREFORE ART THOU" INSTEAD OF JUST
> "WHY"?
> WHY CAN'T YOU SPEAK SIMPLY, OR ARE YOU JUST SHY?
> SADLY YOUR VOCABULARY'S OFTEN FOUND IN
> CAPILLARIES.

JULIET. It's Capulet.

ROMEO. *(gestures, "don't interrupt")*
> BUT WHY "WHEREFORE ARE THOU?" INSTEAD OF JUST
> "WHY"?
> I HAVE THIS FRIEND MERCUTIO.
> HE HAS HIS OWN BIZARRE LINGO.
> PLEASE DON'T GO AND BE LIKE HIM
> AND USE ARCHAIC SYNONYMS.
> I LAUGH AT HIS JOKES BUT I DON'T UNDERSTAND.
> I BOUGHT THE *CLIFF NOTES* — I DO WHAT I CAN!
> SO WHY "WHEREFORE ART THOU" INSTEAD OF JUST
> "WHY"?
> WHY WOULD WE SAY "PARTING" INSTEAD OF
> "GOODBYE"?
> SO I BEG YOU, JULIET, REIN IN THE POETRY
> FOR I AM JUST A SIMPLE GUY IN LOVE WITH THEE.

JULIET.
> FORGET WHEREFORE FOR I'M IN LOVE WITH THEE.

> *(Song ends. Tableau. They sit on the bench. They giggle as he goes in for a kiss.)*

JULIET. If you want to kiss me, we have to get married.

ROMEO. Yeah, okay.

> *(They run off.)*

31. INT. DUNGEON

FRIAR LAURENCE. I think he was saying, "Okay," so he could get laid. But when he came to me, he was very sincere.[23]

---

23 See Appendix 6 for alternate lyrics and dialogue.

PRINCE. This is where it gets complicated.

FRIAR LAURENCE. Yes, I was picking flowers….

(As the FRIAR stands, the scene transforms…)

32. INT. FRIAR LAURENCE'S CELL

(FRIAR LAURENCE picks flowers. ROMEO enters.)

ROMEO. Good morrow, Father.

FRIAR LAURENCE. Gwaa! Don't hurt me, I swear she came onto me.

(realizes)

Romeo, my boy, you're up early this morning.

ROMEO. Am I?

(Doddering FRIAR JOHN, played by the actor who plays BENVOLIO, enters. FRIAR JOHN has about 20 years on FRIAR LAURENCE.)

FRIAR LAURENCE. What ho, Friar John.

ROMEO. Hi, Friar John.

FRIAR JOHN. Romeo, we missed you at the church carnival last night. We made 50,000 ducats at the baptismal clown-dunking booth.

FRIAR LAURENCE. That's great. I might make that a weekly event. Good work on that, Friar John.

FRIAR JOHN. Good, good. Hub hub.

(FRIAR JOHN and exits.)

ROMEO. What a curious little man.

FRIAR LAURENCE. You think so, too?

ROMEO. Oh, boy, Friar, I'll tell you what, those roses are beautiful.

FRIAR LAURENCE. Oh, thank you.

ROMEO. *(happily confident)* Uh, you know, a rose with another name is still the same thing.

FRIAR LAURENCE. I never thought of it like that. Nicely said, Romeo.

ROMEO. Aren't those the kind of flowers you can distill into poisons and knockout drugs?

FRIAR LAURENCE. Maybe. Say, you're mighty carefree. Wait a minute, you didn't get to bed, did you?

ROMEO. That last is true – the sweeter rest was mine.

FRIAR LAURENCE. God pardon sin! Were you with Rosaline?

ROMEO. She is so fifteen minutes ago.

(**ROMEO** *sings #14, a reprise of "Beautiful Day."*)

IT'S A BEAUTIFUL DAY IN VERONA!
I'VE BEEN FEASTING WITH THE ENEMY,

FRIAR LAURENCE. The enemy? What are you talkin' about?

ROMEO.

I'M KINDA ON THE FENCE ABOUT
THE HOUSE OF CAPULET.
BUT JULIET'S THE ONE FOR ME.

FRIAR LAURENCE.   Juliet?

ROMEO.

IT'S A BEAUTIFUL DAY IN VERONA!
C'MON, LET'S HAVE A BEER.

FRIAR LAURENCE.

                    NOT BEFORE NINE.
HOLY SAINTS, WHAT A CHANGE IS HERE!

ROMEO.

I BELONG TO JULIET AND SHE IS MINE.

ROMEO & FRIAR LAURENCE.

OH, IT'S A BEAUTIFUL DAY IN VERONA!
WHO THE HELL IS ROSALINE?

(*They end with a hilarious four beat dance.*)

FRIAR LAURENCE. So it's out with Rosaline, in with Juliet Capulet?

ROMEO. You told me to forget Rosaline, and I have.

FRIAR LAURENCE. What's that sound? Oh, I know, it's the echo of your cries from yesterday!

ROMEO. Marry us.

FRIAR LAURENCE. Holy shit![24]

ROMEO. Friar, we're in a house of God.

FRIAR LAURENCE. That I sweep and mop so I can say what I want. You wanna get married!? Could we please have some middle ground between Sad Romeo and Insane Romeo?

(The **FRIAR** *sings #15, "You Must Be Crazy," a reprise of "Trouble.")*

YOU MUST BE CRAZY.

ROMEO.

BUT I–

FRIAR LAURENCE.

LOVE HER.

YOU'RE CORRUPTED BY HER PULCHRITUDE.

A MARRIAGE–

ROMEO.

YES!

FRIAR LAURENCE.

HUSH,

I AM THINKING,

COULD ELIMINATE THE FAMILY FEUD.

AND THE SURVEY WOULD SAY "FRIAR LAURENCE GAVE HOPE.

HE'S PRACTIC'LY ANOTHER SAINT JUDE."

NORMALLY THE FAM'LY'S ENDORSEMENT IS SOUGHT

BUT IN THIS CASE WE'VE GOT LATITUDE.

*(***ROMEO** *dances and claps his hands in this section.)*

I'LL GET PROMOTED.

MAYBE TO BISHOP.

LIKE THE BURNING BUSH THIS MUST BE A SIGN.

---

24 See Appendix 6 for alternate lyrics and dialogue.

(ROMEO and the FRIAR display a flair for patty-cake.)

FRIAR LAURENCE. *(cont.)*
IF I DO "I DO'S"
FOR THE TWO OF YOUSE,
COULD THE RANK OF CARDINAL BE FAR BEHIND?

ROMEO. Sweet!

(ROMEO grapevines off and the FRIAR...)

33. INT. DUNGEON

(...sings in the dungeon with the PRINCE.)

FRIAR LAURENCE.
ANYWAY, THAT WAS MY THINKING
WHEN I SAID I WOULD OFFICIATE.
REALLY I JUST WANTED MORE BUTTS IN THE PEWS
AND COLD CASH IN THE COLLECTION PLATE.

PRINCE. In retrospect, you think that was a good plan?

FRIAR. Yes. No.

PRINCE. Maybe you should have, oh, I don't know, let the parents in on that idea. Or does God's will trump parental authority?

FRIAR. I really thought it was the best thing to do at the time.

PRINCE. C'mon. Giving them dime bags would have been more productive. And what about Pre-Cana? Or didn't they teach you that in priest school?

FRIAR. No, they taught us.

PRINCE. I wish you'd have been my priest. My wife and I had to meet with other couples for three fuckin' months.[25]

(As the PRINCE exits, the scene transforms to...)

---

[25] See Appendix 6 for alternate lyrics and dialogue

34. EXT. A STREET IN VERONA – THE NEXT DAY

(MERCUTIO and BENVOLIO enter. Occasionally MERCUTIO manipulates his stuffed animal to nod and shake its head.)

BENVOLIO. Tybalt has sent a challenge and Romeo will answer it.

MERCUTIO. Don't you see, man? Romeo's already dead. The very pin of his heart cleft with the blind bow-boy's butt shaft. Is he the man to encounter Tybalt? *(MERCUTIO practices outlandish fencing moves.)* Ah, the immortal passado, the punto reverso, the hay.

BENVOLIO. The what?

MERCUTIO. The –

(ROMEO enters.)

ROMEO. Hey.

MERCUTIO. Without his roe, like a dried herring: O flesh, flesh, how art thou fishified!

(ROMEO laughs like he understands. The second MERCUTIO turns to BENVOLIO, ROMEO stops laughing. BENVOLIO laughs like he understands. When MERCUTIO turns to ROMEO, ROMEO laughs and BENVOLIO stops. Eventually, ROMEO crosses to the bench mouthing "What the hell?")

Hey, you gave us the slip last night.

ROMEO. Well, my business was great, and in such a case as mine a man may strain courtesy.

MERCUTIO. Oooh, I can't think of a comeback, come between us, Benvolio.

(The NURSE and GREGORY enter.)

NURSE. I must speak to Romeo.

ROMEO. I'm Romeo.

MERCUTIO. This is the girl you met last night? I can see why the bawdy hand of the dial is now upon the prick of noon.

NURSE. Excuse me?

ROMEO. He's saying, sarcastically, Nurse, that you're so beautiful he can understand why a man would be aroused in your presence.

MERCUTIO. I'm not being sarcastic. Good stuff.

(**ROMEO** *grabs the stuffed animal and throws it off.*)

MERCUTIO. Leonard!

(**MERCUTIO** *exits.*)

ROMEO. He just loves to hear himself talk.

NURSE. I think I might like to hear more of it. Gregory, keep watch. If any of these young men try to take advantage of me, go away.

(**GREGORY** *exits.*)

Romeo, my lady has asked me to make certain inquiries about your character and what your intentions are.

BENVOLIO. He won't two-time her like he did Rosaline.

NURSE. Two-time?

(**ROMEO** *throws* **BENVOLIO**'s *hat offstage.*)

BENVOLIO. My hat has been blown off by the wind.

(**BENVOLIO** *exits.*)

ROMEO. I don't know who that was.

NURSE. I warn you, if you double deal Juliet I will mess you up so bad.

ROMEO. Bid her devise some means to come to shrift this afternoon, and there she shall at Friar Laurence's cell be shriv'd and married. Here is for thy pains.

NURSE. I am the wind!

*(Borne on the wings of a piano gliss, the **NURSE** leaps off right and **ROMEO** leaps off left.)*

35. INT. JULIET'S CHAMBER – LATER THE SAME DAY

JULIET. The clock strook nine when I did send the nurse. In half an hour she promised to return. Perchance she cannot meet him — that's not so. O, she is so lame!

*(A breathless **NURSE**, assisted by **GREGORY**, enters.)*

Oh, God, she comes! Nurse, did you meet with him, what news.

NURSE. I'm not a runner, Juliet, I'm just not a runner, that's what news. Stay near, Gregory, in case some of those young men want to take advantage of me.

*(**GREGORY** exits. **NURSE** sits down, really out of breath.)*

JULIET. Okay, what did Romeo say about our marriage?

NURSE. Oh, my back, my back, I can't get proper shoes and that just effects the whole spinal column, oh, oh.

*(**JULIET** massages her shoulders, then uses a chopping technique on her back.)*

I have a sudden chopping sensation in my back. AHHH! I think I have a migraine.

JULIET. Sweet, sweet, sweet, sweet nurse: shut up and tell me, what news of my love?

NURSE. Juliet, where is your mother?

JULIET. Where is my mother? She's right here, Nurse, because I want her to hear all about this. She'll be so happy. I DON'T KNOW WHERE SHE IS.

NURSE. Oh, my heart, my heart.

 (a Redd Foxx bit)

 Jerry, I'm coming, it's the big one.

JULIET. Did you talk to Romeo or not?

NURSE. Yes, he says – he says go to Friar and be married today.

JULIET. Nurse, get a ladder and put it beneath my window for Romeo to climb.

NURSE. Sure, I'm old, I've got a bad back, I'll just drag a ladder underneath your window. That won't look suspicious.

JULIET. Hie to high fortune! My love awaits.

 (As JULIET joyously dashes away, the orchestra continues #16 and...)

36. INT. DUNGEON/FRIAR LAURENCE'S CELL

 (...the PRINCE and ROMEO enter. The FRIAR finds himself in the eye of a chromatic maelstrom.)

PRINCE. So you just decided to listen to a teenage boy and let him marry his fourteen year-old girlfriend. Good.

 (The PRINCE exits.)

37. INT. FRIAR LAURENCE'S CHURCH

 (ROMEO and JULIET kneel at the altar as #16 "Our Town Underscore" continues. The FRIAR uses a New England accent.)

FRIAR LAURENCE. There are a lot of things to be said about a wedding. We can't get them all into one wedding, naturally, and especially not into a wedding at Grover's Corners, Italy, where they're awfully plain and short. In this wedding, I play the minister. That gives me the right to say a few more things about it. Y'see, some churches say that marriage is a sacrament. I don't quite know what that means because the state says marriage is a legal contract in which the woman is property. Well, that's my sermon. Romeo, do you take Juliet….

(FRIAR LAURENCE continues mouthing the sermon silently. Neither he nor JULIET notices ROMEO speaking his thoughts.)

ROMEO. I wish I were back at school…I don't want to get married.

(MRS. GIBBS from Our Town enters.)

MRS. GIBBS. George, what's the matter?

ROMEO. Ma, I don't want to grow old. Why's everybody pushing me so?

MRS. GIBBS. Why, George, you wanted it.

ROMEO. I wanted to get laid. Why do I have to get married at all? Listen, Ma, for the last time I ask you.[26]

MRS. GIBBS. No, you're a man now…and I want to be alone with your father.

(MRS. GIBBS exits.)

FRIAR LAURENCE. So long as you both shall live?

ROMEO. I do.

FRIAR LAURENCE. Juliet, do you take Romeo, to have…

JULIET. I've never felt so alone in my whole life. And look at George over there, looking so. *(ROMEO makes a ridiculous face.)* I hate him. I wish I were dead. Papa, Papa!

(MR. WEBB from Our Town enters.)

MR. WEBB. Emily, now don't get upset.

JULIET. But, Papa, I don't want to get married.

---

26 See Appendix 6 for alternate lyrics and dialogue.

MR. WEBB. Sh, sh. Emily, everything's all right.

JULIET. Why can't I stay for a while just as I am? Let's go away. Don't you remember you used to say all the time that I was *your* girl.

MR. WEBB. When you say it like that, it sounds so sick. George, I'm giving away my daughter. Do you think you can take care of her?

ROMEO. Mr. Webb, I want to try.

FRIAR LAURENCE. No one is listening to me.

JULIET. All I want is someone to love me.

ROMEO. I will, Emily.

 (**MR. WEBB** *kisses* **JULIET** *way too romantically.*)[27]

MR. WEBB. You kids have fun.

 (**MR. WEBB** *exits.*)

FRIAR LAURENCE. Then by the power invested in me by the states of Verona and New Hampshire, I secretly pronounce you man and wife.

ROMEO. Huzzah!

 (**ROMEO** *and* **JULIET** *exit right as "The Wedding March" resolves hastily. The* **FRIAR** *exits down left as the lights change.*)

38. EXT. THE STREET IN VERONA

(Benvolio and Mercutio enter up center.)

BENVOLIO. There's always a fight on this street. I don't know why we bother to come this way.

MERCUTIO. Thou art like one of those fellows that, when he enters the confines of a tavern, claps his sword upon the table, and says, 'God send me no need of thee!' and by the operation of the second cup draws him on the drawer, when indeed there is no need.

---

27 See Appendix 6 for alternate lyrics and dialogue.

BENVOLIO. What the hell are you talking about?

MERCUTIO. Come, come, thou art as hot a Jack in thy mood as any in Italy and as soon mov'd to be moody, and as soon moody to be mov'd.

BENVOLIO. Badges? We don't need no stinkin' badges.

MERCUTIO. What the hell are you talking about?

BENVOLIO. Welcome to my world!

(**TYBALT** *enters with his sword drawn.*)

TYBALT. Mercutio!

MERCUTIO & BENVOLIO. *(singing)*
> WHAT HO! TYBALT!

TYBALT. Thou consort'st with Romeo.

MERCUTIO. Consort?

TYBALT. You're a fag.[28]

MERCUTIO. 'Zounds, consort! Though I do prefer the frankfurter to the taco, 'tis not a subject fit for jest!

(*Swords are drawn.* **ROMEO** *enters.*)

ROMEO. Love, exciting and new, come aboard, we're expect – Hi, you guys. Hey, Tybalt, s'up?

(**TYBALT** *begins #17, "Here's the One I'm After."*)

TYBALT.
> THERE'S THE ONE I'M AFTER!
> AT LAST I CAN KILL YOU.
> YOU VILLAINOUS PILL WHO
> IS THE REASON I EVEN LEARNED TO FENCE.

ROMEO.
> ACCEPT MY APOLOGY.
> I LOVE YOU, SO DON'T KILL ME.
> BESIDES, THE PRINCE OUTLAWED BELLIGERENCE.

MERCUTIO.
> ROMEO, LOVE HAS MADE YOU WEAK
> AND I CAN SEE YOUR COWARD'S STREAK.
> IT IS TIME WE FULFILL OUR DESTINIES.

---

28 See Appendix 6 for alternate lyrics and dialogue.

MERCUTIO & TYBALT.

> JUST LET ME KILL HIM....PRETTY PLEASE.

> *(**MERCUTIO** and **TYBALT** draw.)*

MERCUTIO & TYBALT. Hah!

ROMEO. Calm down! Can't we talk about this?

TYBALT. Talk?! Why don't we start a book club? You're even less of a man than I thought you were.

MERCUTIO. Here I am fighting in your place and you're saying calm down and play nice.

BENVOLIO. That's the first time I ever understood you!

ROMEO. Fighting never solved anything.

> *(SLOW MOTION.* **TYBALT** *stabs* **MERCUTIO** *under* **ROMEO**'s *arm. REGULAR MOTION.* **TYBALT** *says childishly...)*

TYBALT. Ha ha ha ha ha!

> *(**TYBALT** flees. **MERCUTIO** sings #18, "Oh, What a Pity I'm Dead.")*

MERCUTIO.

> HEED MY ADVICE. DON'T HAVE YOUR HEART
> SLICED IN TWO BY YOUNG TYBALT'S BLADE.
> EVERYONE DIES BUT I ALWAYS THOUGHT
> AN EXCEPTION FOR ME WOULD BE MADE.
> A PLAGUE ON BOTH YOUR HOUSES.
> YOU OUGHT TO BE DYING INSTEAD!
> I HAD THE WHOLE WORLD BUT I LOST MY SOUL.
> QUICK GET A BIBLE AND LOOK FOR LOOPHOLES.
> SO LONG, FAREWELL, AUF WIEDERSEHEN.
> TAKE ME TO CLARKSVILLE TO GET THE LAST
> TRAIN.
> OH, WHAT A PITY....THAT I'M DEAD!

> *(**MERCUTIO** dies. Leonard the bear enters sadly to a sample of "Il Pagliacci."*

BENVOLIO. Don't look, Leonard!

(Leonard exits.)

ROMEO. Mercutio dead! I thought all for the best.

(Lights change.)

39. INT. DUNGEON

FRIAR LAURENCE. If only it had ended there.

PRINCE. Yes, if only. But Tybalt came back!

FRIAR LAURENCE. And for no fucking reason![29]

(Lights change, but FRIAR and PRINCE remain on and watch the following.)

40. EXT. THE STREET IN VERONA

(TYBALT returns, confronting ROMEO and BENVO-LIO.)

TYBALT. I got a memo from Fate and it says I am supposed to come back on.

(ROMEO stabs TYBALT.)

Ow…OWWW! A hit, a hit, a palpable hit.

(He falls down dead. ROMEO and BENVOLIO "cheese it.")

41. INT. DUNGEON/FLASHBACKS/THE STREET

(The noisy MOB sweeps the stage. Note: The JULIET actress returns as SAMPSON. The ROMEO actor plays ANOTHER GUY.)

PRINCE. The mob is getting unruly.

---

[29] See Appendix 6 for alternate lyrics and dialogue.

(Angry individuals pop on and off from various entrances.)

MOB 3 (BENVOLIO). He introduced them.

FRIAR LAURENCE. That's not true!

MOB 2 (CAPULET). He put words in Romeo's mouth!

FRIAR LAURENCE. That's not true.

MOB 1 (LADY CAPULET). He married them!

FRIAR LAURENCE. Okay, that I did do.

PRINCE. You know, I'm gonna add the murders of Mercutio and Tybalt to this.

FRIAR LAURENCE. Why?

MOB 5 (TYBALT). Friar Laurence was the one who pushed me back on stage.

FRIAR LAURENCE. That's impossible, I was over there!

PRINCE. One thing leads to another. Plus this mob is out for blood.

(The mob re-enters and sings #19, "Friar Laurence's Fault.")

MOB 2 (CAPULET).
TYBALT KILLED MERCUTIO.

MOB 1 (LADY CAPULET).
HEAVEN HELP THE SAINTS PRESERVE US.

MOB 3 (BENVOLIO).
PERSONALLY I THINK IT WAS
A SORT OF PUBLIC SERVICE.

MOB 4 (MONTAGUE).
BUT ROMEO STABBED TYBALT.

MOB 5 (TYBALT).
THAT'S MURDER AND ASSAULT.

ALL.
AND THE ONE THING THAT IS OBVIOUS: IT'S FRIAR LAURENCE'S FAULT!

*(The **PRINCE** and **FRIAR** remain left. **MONTAGUE** and **CAPULET** take center.)*

CAPULET.

I DETEST LORD MONTAGUE,

MONTAGUE.

AND I HATE CAPULET.

CAPULET.

THE FRICTION IS NO FICTION
BUT THE REASON WE FORGET.

MONTAGUE.

THERE WAS SOMETHING WITH MY COUSIN

CAPULET.

AND A GUY NAMED UNCLE WALT.

(The rest of the mob re-enters.)

ALL.

BUT ONE THING THAT IS OBVIOUS:
IT'S FRIAR LAURENCE'S FAULT!

*(Modulation as they all ad lib rumors. They form a
big rotating clump and the **FRIAR** revolves around
it.)*

MOB 7 (ANOTHER GUY).

THEN THERE WAS THAT EARTHQUAKE
A COUPLE YEARS AGO.

MOB 5 (TYBALT).

AND EARLIER THIS SUMMER I SWEAR I SAW IT SNOW.

MOB 1 (LADY CAPULET).

STOP THE FIENDISH FRIAR
AND BRING HIS SORCERY TO A HALT.

PRINCE.

IT SOUNDS LIKE YOU'RE RESPONSIBLE.

ALL.

IT'S FRIAR LAURENCE'S FAULT!

*(Modulation. The **MOB** forms two columns.)*

MOB 6 (SAMPSON). Philistine!

MOB 5 (TYBALT). Heretic!

MOB 3 (BENVOLIO). Infidel!

MOB 7 (ANOTHER GUY). Jerk!

(The FRIAR is surrounded and pushed around.)

MOB 2 (LADY CAPULET).

BRUTUS STABBED CAESAR,

AT LEAST THAT'S WHAT THEY SAY.

MOB 6 (SAMPSON).

BUT WHERE WAS FRIAR LAURENCE

ON THAT ROMAN HOLIDAY?

MOB 7 (ROMEO).

THERE'S SODOM AND GOMORRAH

WHERE LOT'S WIFE TURNED TO SALT.

FRIAR LAURENCE.

YOU'RE JUST MAKING THE ME SCAPEGOAT HERE FOR

EVERYTHING!

ALL.

IT'S FRIAR LAURENCE'S FAULT!

(They all leap at him. He escapes and stands on a bench, which has been moved up center.)

FRIAR LAURENCE.

I PROTEST YOUR LEAP IN LOGIC.

MOB 2 (LADY CAPULET).

HE CAUSED THE PLAGUE BUBONIC.

ALL.

IT'S FRIAR LAURENCE'S FAULT!

FRIAR LAURENCE. You've got to believe me, I'm innocent!

MOB 6 (SOPRANO).

BECAUSE OF HIM THERE'S ORIGINAL SIN.

(Blackout.)

End of Act One

ACT TWO

42. EXT. A STREET IN VERONA/INT. DUNGEON

(Lights bump up. All sing #20, "Act Two Opener" in the positions we saw them last.)

ALL.

IT'S FRIAR LAURENCE'S FAULT!

*(All exit but the **PRINCE** and the **FRIAR**. Crossfade to the dungeon light.)*

FRIAR LAURENCE. It is *not* all my fault. I didn't banish Romeo to Mantua. You did.

PRINCE. That was the best legal solution available to me at the time. What was I supposed to do?

FRIAR LAURENCE. I don't know. Have him pick up trash along the Appian Way. But when you banished him, that just made everything worse.

(Lights change.)

43. INT. JULIET'S CHAMBER

*(Blissfully ignorant **JULIET** runs on and looks out her window.)*

JULIET. What a beautiful day in Verona! I've never been so happy in all my life. And yet there's a funeral procession.

TOWN CRIER. *(offstage)* Make way for the body of Tybalt.

JULIET. Wow. And I also know someone named Tybalt. It just makes you think about how humankind is all connected.

(The **NURSE** *enters.)*

NURSE. Juliet, Juliet, it's terrible…

JULIET. Oh, Nurse, I have a feeling things will fall into place for everyone. Call it God's will, call it feminine intuition, call it wishful thinking, but I just know Father will get into a 12-step program. You, Nurse, will meet a doctor. Or at least a dentist. Romeo will have a barrow in the marketplace. I'll become a singer in the band. With a couple of kids we will build a home sweet home.

NURSE. Tybalt is dead.

JULIET. Yes, I know. Isn't it weird that we know someone named Tybalt, too?

NURSE. It is your cousin Tybalt that is dead.

JULIET. *(sing-screams - see #21.)*

WHAAAAAT?

NURSE. Romeo killed him.

JULIET.

WHAAAAAT?

NURSE. The Prince has banished Romeo to Mantua.

JULIET.

WHAAAAAT?

(She weeps.)

NURSE. Oh, you poor little girl. How you must be torn. Your cousin killed by your lover.

JULIET. To be honest, I'm more upset about Romeo.

NURSE. You are 60% upset about Romeo and 40% about Tybalt.

JULIET. All I remember about Tybalt is him making fun of me and drinking too much.

NURSE. So it's 75% about Romeo and –

JULIET. It's 99% about Romeo and 1% about the rest of the pain in the world, and Tybalt is in there somewhere.

NURSE. The Friar has given Romeo sanctuary, but he must leave Verona or face execution.

(**JULIET** *reprises "Why Wherefore" as #21, "Take My Ring to Romeo."*)

JULIET.
TAKE MY RING TO ROMEO.

NURSE. What?

JULIET.
TELL HIM NOT TO DESPAIR.
TONIGHT HE CAN VISIT ME
BUT TO USE THE BACK STAIR.
AT FIRST IT WAS MY CLEVER PLOY
TO SIMPLY USE THAT HANDSOME BOY.
BUT I'VE MESSED THAT UP
BY FALLING IN LOVE.
NOW I'M SIMPLY OVERWHELMED.
I'M LIKE A SHIP WITHOUT A HELM.
OUR FORTUNES CHANGE JUST LIKE THE WIND
OR GOD HAS GOT SOME PETTY WHIMS.
I HIDE MY FEELINGS THE BEST THAT I CAN.
I CAN'T HELP MYSELF. I LOVE THAT MAN!
SO HURRY TO ROMEO.
DID I GIVE YOU THE RING?

NURSE.   Yes.

JULIET.
TONIGHT HE CAN VISIT ME
AND TOGETHER WE'LL SING
A MELODY EXTR'ORDINARY.

NURSE.
YOU'RE WRITING YOUR OBITUARY.

JULIET. I don't care.

JUST BRING HIM BACK TO ME!

(As she holds the last note for a long time, she gestures dramatically, as if she's attached to an Evita machine. Lights to blue.)

44. INT. FRIAR LAURENCE'S CELL

*(**FRIAR LAURENCE** considers **ROMEO**, who weeps profusely.)*

FRIAR LAURENCE. I take it we're back to Sad Romeo.

ROMEO. Banished!

FRIAR LAURENCE. That's right, you've been banished to Mantua.

ROMEO. Don't say that word.

FRIAR LAURENCE. What word, "Mantua?"

ROMEO. No, "banished." 'Tis a fate more terrible than death. Do not name the scoundrel "banishment."

FRIAR LAURENCE. Romeo, what's in a name? You're exiled, you're banished –

ROMEO. Ahhhh —

FRIAR LAURENCE. What?

ROMEO. You said the word!

FRIAR LAURENCE. The Prince was merciful. He could have invoked the death penalty.

ROMEO. How was he merciful?

FRIAR LAURENCE. He merely banished you.

ROMEO. Aaaah! The word! The word! It's torture, not mercy, when Juliet is here in heaven and men and women and cats and dogs and flies can look upon her but I can't because – because —

*(By this time, **ROMEO** can only sputter a mess of "B's.")*

FRIAR LAURENCE. – because you're banished.

ROMEO. Aaahh! You profess to be my friend! Why do you mangle me with that word.

FRIAR LAURENCE. All right, we won't say that word anymore.

(pause)

ROMEO. Aaaah! It's as if in the not-saying you said it.

(two knocks offstage, supplied by MAN 2 or MAN 3)

Aaahh!

FRIAR LAURENCE. What is it now?

ROMEO. The two knocks were not unlike the two syllables of the word.

FRIAR LAURENCE. Knock it off…Hello, who is it?

(The NURSE's hand, holding her signature handkercheif, appears.)

Oh, hello, Nurse.

(The FRIAR kisses the NURSE's hand and exits. Note: the extra hands requisite for the scene are those of the actor who's about the same height as the FRIAR/NURSE actor.)

NURSE. *(offstage)* Friar, I must talk to Romeo.

FRIAR LAURENCE. *(offstage)* It's not really a good time. He's drunk in his own tears.

NURSE. *(offstage)* Oh, it's the same with Juliet.

FRIAR LAURENCE. *(offstage)* Nurse, have you done something different with your wig?

NURSE. *(offstage)* Oh, Friar!

FRIAR LAURENCE. *(offstage)* Come right this way.

NURSE. *(offstage)* I must speak with him alone.

FRIAR LAURENCE. *(offstage)* Okay.

(As the NURSE enters, she is touched by the FRIAR.)

NURSE. You keep watch.

(The **FRIAR** *gives her thumbs up.)*

ROMEO. Nurse! What news of Juliet!?

NURSE. O, she says nothing but weeps and weeps and now falls on her bed, and then starts up, and then falls down again. She mourns your banishment.

ROMEO. AAAH! She mourns both me and Tybalt!

NURSE. It's 99% percent about –

ROMEO. *(pulling out a sword)* I have distressed her! Tell me in what vile part of this anatomy doth my name lodge.

NURSE. Put down that sword! Hi-yah!

(With a quick karate chop the **NURSE** *disarms him.* **ROMEO** *crumples to the floor.)*

ROMEO. Ah, my knuckles!

*(***NURSE** *runs off.)*

NURSE. Friar!

FRIAR LAURENCE. *(offstage)* What's going on in there?

NURSE. *(offstage)* He tried to kill himself.

FRIAR LAURENCE. *(offstage)* He did what? Outta my way.

(He re-enters as the **NURSE** *touches his shoulder. Note: In the following speech, feel free to change "Joliet" to something that makes sense locally.)*

Look, Romeo, knock it off. Your tears are womanish. You killed the most obnoxious man on earth, so you ought to be proud of that. Just stay in Mantua, which is like 10 miles away. It's not like you're going to Joliet. It's more like you're going to summer school. Eventually you can get a pardon from the Prince, everything's gonna work out. More importantly, Juliet is alive. Go get thee to thy love as was decreed. Ascend her chamber hence and comfort her.

ROMEO. Comfort —?

FRIAR LAURENCE. Nudge, nudge, wink, wink.

ROMEO. Say no more, Friar!

FRIAR LAURENCE. Nurse, tell Juliet that Romeo is coming!

(**FRIAR** *exits.*)

NURSE. *(offstage)* What good counsel you gave to Romeo there. I could have stayed and listened to you all night.

FRIAR LAURENCE. *(offstage)* Oh, pshaw.

(*The* **NURSE** *re-enters.*)

NURSE. All right, Romeo — (*The* **FRIAR** *gooses her.*) Friar! Romeo, here is Juliet's ring. Go to Juliet, it is late!

(*She exits.*)

(*offstage*) Goodbye, Friar.

FRIAR LAURENCE. *(offstage)* Okay, goodbye, Nurse *(he enters, then notices she has extended her hand for a kiss)*…oh, goodbye.

(*Now he embraces her for a long kiss. We can see her arms wrapped around his neck. He waves goodbye.* **ROMEO** *bawls.*)

FRIAR LAURENCE. What is it now?

ROMEO. I didn't know we were supposed to bring a gift.

FRIAR LAURENCE. Knock it off.

(**ROMEO** *runs off.* **FRIAR** *crosses into…*)

45. INT. DUNGEON

FRIAR LAURENCE. Yes, I offered Romeo sanctuary, that's legal.

PRINCE. Yes, that's all in the Capulet deposition.

(*to audience*)

PRINCE. *(cont.)* This ought to show young people to be honest with their parents. If Juliet would have told her mother that she was in love with Romeo, her mother might have been angry, but she would have accepted her daughter.

FRIAR LAURENCE. Or killed her!

PRINCE. Or killed her. Either way, she dies.

FRIAR LAURENCE. You don't care either way. You just want to stay in power.

PRINCE. Bingo. The whole point of me being in power is I get to interpret the law so it supports my policy. A lot of this is smoke and mirrors. I make people think it's over and then I smack 'em with "new information" or "startling revelations." In the case of war, it's the "secret weapon." I have to be sensitive to perception.

(They sing #22 "You Understand." Note: depending on the talents of the cast, The **PRINCE** *can accompany the song on guitar,* **GREGORY** *can be "summoned" to accompany them, or another actor can acocmpany them from offstage.)*

PRINCE. *(verse)*

YOU UNDERSTAND THE CRAP THAT I ENDURE
EVERY SINGLE DAY I'M ON THE THRONE.
FROM IMMIGRANTS ARE TAKING ALL THE JOBS
TO CONGESTION IN THE RESIDENTIAL ZONES.
PEOPLE LOVE A FIGHT THAT'S BLACK AND WHITE
'CAUSE EVERYTHING'S A BIG GREY AREA.
IF PEOPLE KNEW HOW MESSED UP OUR NATION IS,
THEY'D ALL SUCCUMB TO MASS HYSTERIA.

(chorus)

THOUGH LEGALLY WE'RE ENEMIES MOST BITTER,
MY ADMIRATION FOR YOU IS COMPLETE.
I LIKE YOU SO I'D LIKE TO SEE YOU SET FREE
BUT I CAN'T FIND A WAY THAT'S DISCREET.
YOU UNDERSTAND.

FRIAR LAURENCE.

(verse)

YOU UNDERSTAND THAT WE'RE A LOT ALIKE
FOR I AM ALSO WEARY OF COMPLAINTS.

PRINCE & FRIAR LAURENCE.

EVERYONE I COUNSEL IS A WHINER

FRIAR LAURENCE.

WHO WONDERS WHY THEY'VE NOT BEEN MADE A
SAINT.
THE CROWD OUTSIDE CLAMORS FOR MY HEAD
IF I DO OR DON'T MAKE A CONFESSION.
AS LONG AS I'M CAPTURED IN YOUR CASTLE KEEP
IT KEEPS THEIR MINDS OFF THE RECESSION.

PRINCE & FRIAR LAURENCE.

(chorus)

THOUGH LEGALLY WE'RE ENEMIES MOST BITTER,

FRIAR LAURENCE.

GOD'S LAW SAYS TURN THE OTHER CHEEK.
I LIKE YOU SO I'D LIKE TO SEE ME SET FREE
EVEN IF YOU KINDA SORTA CHEAT.
YOU UNDERSTAND.

PRINCE & FRIAR LAURENCE.

(bridge)

WE ARE TWO PILLARS IN A GREAT CATHEDRAL
SUPPORTING THE CEILING, OUR STATE.

PRINCE.

IT'S MORE LIKE VERONA'S A PATIENT
AND YOU'RE A LIMB I MUST AMPUTATE.

(short verse)

UNDERSTAND THIS ISN'T ABOUT YOU
EVEN WHEN I SAY THAT IT IS.
YOU'RE MY WEAPON OF MASS DISTRACTION
AND A LOT OF THIS IS SHOW BIZ.

PRINCE & FRIAR LAURENCE.

(chorus)

THOUGH LEGALLY WE'RE ENEMIES MOST BITTER,
WE BOTH WANT TO DO WHAT IS RIGHT.

PRINCE.

WHAT'S RIGHT IS WHAT KEEPS ME IN POWER,

PRINCE & FRIAR LAURENCE.

WHAT'S WRONG KEEPS ME UP AT NIGHT.

FRIAR LAURENCE.

YOU UNDERSTAND.

PRINCE.

YOU UNDERSTAND.

FRIAR LAURENCE.

YOU UNDERSTAND.

PRINCE.

YOU UNDERSTAND.

PRINCE & FRIAR LAURENCE.

YOU UNDERSTAND.

(Lights change as they relinquish the stage. Immediate musical transition to...)

46. EXT/INT. JULIET'S BALCONY/JULIET'S CHAMBER – SAME NIGHT

(ROMEO *shows up beneath the balcony. He and* **JULIET** *immediately segue into #23 "We're the Ones Who Started It All.")*

BOTH.

OUR LOVE IS ORIGINAL,
SO RARE AND SO TRUE,
IT'S TRULY ONE OF A KIND.
I CAN ONLY BEST DESCRIBE
WHAT I FEEL INSIDE
AS THE GREATEST LOVE OF ALL TIME.

ROMEO. *(verse)*

WE'RE LIKE DESI ARNAZ

JULIET.

AND HIS WIFE LUCILLE BALL.

ROMEO.

WE'RE *WHEN HARRY MET SALLY*

JULIET.

WHICH IS LIKE *ANNIE HALL.*

BOTH.

(chorus)

BUT WE'RE NOT LIKE THEM,
THEY'RE US WATERED DOWN.
OUR LOVE WAS "VERBOTEN"
WHEN THEY WEREN'T AROUND.
WE'RE THE ONES WHO STARTED IT ALL.

JULIET.

(verse)

YOU ARE MY LANCELOT.

ROMEO.

YOU'RE MY GUENIVERE.

JULIET.

I'M DORIS DAY

BOTH.

AND THOUGH ROCK WAS QUEER,
(chorus)

OUR LOVE IS SOMETHING
THE WHOLE WORLD ACCEPTS.
TRACY AND HEPBURN SEND ROYALTY CHECKS.
WE'RE THE ONES WHO STARTED IT ALL.

(bridge)

WE'RE OWED A BIG DEBT
FROM DOCTOR ZHIVAGO,
THE MOOR, DESDEMONA, AND
OL' IAGO.

JULIET.

I'M NORMA JEAN,

ROMEO.

I'M JOLTIN' JOE,

JULIET.

I AM KATE WINSLET.

ROMEO.

SO I'M DICAPRIO.

(They dance but stop to say the name of each couple. Current events will dictate the replacement of the following couples' names. In other words, insert the name of a celebrity who has done something stupid here.)[30]

We're like Demi and Ashton.

JULIET. We're like Frodo and Sam.

ROMEO. We're like Paris Hilton and five guys I know personally.

JULIET.

(sings verse)

JOHN LENNON AND YOKO
FIT THIS CATEGORY.

ROMEO.

LIKE TONY AND MARIA
AND THEIR WEST SIDE STORY.

BOTH.

(chorus)

WE'RE NOT LONG FOR THIS EARTH
SO HERE'S OUR BIG GRIPE.
IT'S US AND NOT THEM
THAT'S LOVE'S ARCHETYPE.
WE'RE THE ONES WHO STARTED IT ALL.

(key change)

---

[30] See Appendix 6 for alternate lyrics and dialogue.

SONNY AND CHER
AIN'T GOT NOTHIN' ON US,
NOR DO CAPTAIN JOHN SMITH
AND HIS POCAHANTAS.

(chorus)

FORGET PRINCESS GRACE
AND HER PRINCE RAINIER
WE SET THE BAR AND WE SET IT UP HERE.
WE'RE THE ONES WHO STARTED IT ALL.
WE'RE THE ONES WHO STARTED IT ALL.

(They dance the last slow dance at the prom as the lights broaden and...)

47. INT. DUNGEON

*(...**FRIAR LAURENCE** and the **PRINCE** observe them.)*

PRINCE. They deserved to die. They had pre-marital sex. That's against God's will.

FRIAR LAURENCE. They were married. I just forgot to send in the paperwork.

PRINCE. They had unsanctified sex.

*(The **PRINCE** exits. The **FRIAR** looks at **ROMEO** and **JULIET** as if to say, "What have I done?")*

ROMEO & JULIET.

WE'RE THE ONES WHO STARTED IT ALL.

(They dance off as...)

48. INT. VILLA CAPULET –
THAT SAME NIGHT

(...the **SERVING WENCH** *and* **CAPULET** *dance on, concluding #23.)*

CAPULET. You're one of the best serving wenches we've got around here.
(pause)

My wife doesn't understand me.

*(***PARIS*** *enters.)*

PARIS. Lord Capulet, I – that is not your wife!

CAPULET. All right, hit the road.

(He slaps the **SERVING WENCH** *on the behind and she exits.)*

This better be good.

PARIS. Lord Capulet, I love your daughter and I want to marry her on Thursday.

CAPULET. Marry my daughter on Thursday? That's way too soon.

(Note: Substitute a local or newsworthy wealthy man for "Lord Pritzker.")

PARIS. Unless I marry Juliet this week, I will sell my vineyard to Lord Pritzker.

CAPULET. Thursday it is.

(They shake hands. **PARIS** *exits, giving the eye to* **LADY CAPULET**, *who enters.)*

LADY CAPULET. What's with you and the serving wench?

CAPULET. Hey. I'm busy drinking.

LADY CAPULET. You drink too much.

CAPULET. You're still here. I don't drink enough.

(Lights change.)

49. INT. JULIET'S CHAMBER – THE NEXT MORNING

(#24, Sitcom musical transition. **ROMEO** *and* **JULIET** *enter.* **ROMEO** *ties his shoe and prepares to depart.)*

ROMEO. Thanks, that was great.

JULIET. *(nonplussed)* Yeah. They have this book on kissing at the library…

ROMEO. Will they have it at the library in Mantua where I'm….where I'm…

JULIET. …banished?

ROMEO. Gwaaa!!

(**LADY CAPULET** *enters*)

LADY CAPULET. Juliet, your father and…Ahhh! *(She trades screams with* **ROMEO**.*)* Deputy Fife, come quick, it's Romeo Montague!

ROMEO. Don't call for the Deputy. He won't come.

LADY CAPULET. Whatever are you talking about?

ROMEO. It's me, Lady Capulet, Barney Fife.

(From off stage, **MAN 2** *"dubs"* **ROMEO***, so it appears* **ROMEO** *is imitating* **BARNEY***.)*

"You don't recognize me because I'm wearing a Romeo mask."

LADY CAPULET. *(#24, continued)* Wow, that's a FANTASTIC MASK!

JULIET. That's what I said. But we heard some Montagues infiltrated the party wearing masks and Deputy Fife here made one in the laboratory.

LADY CAPULET. The laboratory?

ROMEO. Yes, the laboratory. Well, science beckons. Verona, for a while I take my leave.

(He kisses **LADY CAPULET***. She likes it. He kisses* **JULIET***. She likes it a lot. He kisses an audience member.)*

ROMEO. *(cont.)* Ladies.

(He exits, brimming with confidence.)

JULIET. Yes. More like that in the future.

(Pleasure ripples through **JULIET** *from head to toe.)*

LADY CAPULET. Juliet, are you still weeping for Tybalt?

JULIET. Boo hoo. No, I think I'm over it now.

LADY CAPULET. I'm not. And this exile to Mantua is ridiculous. We're sending a man over there to poison the villainous Romeo.

JULIET. What? Mother, that's…a great idea. The way you've chosen to dole out justice when you couldn't get any, well, wow, it makes me proud to be a Capulet. Only someone who feels about that darn Romeo the way I do should mix the potion.

LADY CAPULET. We'll have to ask your father.

JULIET. Better yet, let me go to Mantua on Wednesday and administer the poison myself.

LADY CAPULET. That's a school night.

JULIET. Okay, okay, Thursday.

LADY CAPULET. On Thursday, you're getting married to Paris. So Friday might work.

JULIET. What? I would rather marry Romeo, whom you know I hate, than marry Paris.

(She cries and falls to her bench. **CAPULET** *enters.)*

CAPULET. Oh, in that little body there's a whole ocean of sorrow. Did you tell her yet?

JULIET. I'm too young to get married.

CAPULET. Come now. You are fourteen years old. Most women your age have had two babies by now.

JULIET. I'm too upset about Tybalt to get married!

CAPULET. This will cheer you up.

JULIET. I don't love Paris!

LADY CAPULET. Your father and I are living proof you don't need love.

CAPULET. Don't touch me.

LADY CAPULET. Okay.

JULIET. I want to go to Mantua to poison Romeo.

CAPULET. Not on a school night.

JULIET. *(aside)* The only thing left to do is fake insanity.

CAPULET. And don't try to fake insanity. You're going to get married on Thursday to Paris or I will throw you out, you green-sickness carrion! You baggage! You disobedient wretch!

(The **NURSE** *and* **BARNEY** *sneak in and eavesdrop.)*

LADY CAPULET. Fie, fie, are you mad?

CAPULET. No. This is mad.

(He goes ballistic.)

I MAKE A DECENT LIVING AT WHATEVER IT IS I DO AND PUT FOOD ON THE TABLE AND ALL I GET FROM YOU TWO IS LIP.

NURSE. He's not even drunk!

CAPULET. I heard that, you old skankbag! *(To* **LADY CAPULET***.)* If I'da known this was the kid that was gonna come out of you, I never would have married you.

JULIET. Yeah, well, if I would have known this is the way you were gonna be I would have stayed in.

CAPULET. No more excuses.

LADY CAPULET. Yes, you are looking older by the second.

CAPULET. You are my property and you're going to do as I say.

JULIET. Delay this marriage or make the bridal bed on that dim monument where Tybalt lies.

CAPULET. *(childishly)* Oooh, the suicide threat. I'm soo scared!

(to **NURSE** *and* **BARNEY***)*

Get out of my way or I'll kill you!

(He exits.)

JULIET. Oh, sweet mother, cast me not away.

LADY CAPULET. *(Ignoring* **JULIET**.*)* Hello, Mr. Fife. I'd like to take a tour of your laboratory. Make some masks?

*(***LADY CAPULET*** makes a pass at him and exits.)*

BARNEY. It's the uniform.

(He adjusts himself and follows her.)

JULIET. What am I going to do? How can I marry again unless Romeo dies?

NURSE. Romeo's as good as dead, and Paris is rich and he's rich.

JULIET. I'll go to the Friar to know his remedy.

NURSE. Good idea.

(The scene transforms instantly.)

50. INT. FRIAR LAURENCE'S CELL

(The **NURSE** *becomes the* **FRIAR** *in a bit called "the Nurse-Friar flip." See #24.* **JULIET** *stays.* **PARIS** *hops on.)*

JULIET. Friar.

FRIAR LAURENCE. Yes, it's me. Thursday?

PARIS. Yes.

FRIAR LAURENCE. A lot of people have to work on Thursday.

JULIET. Excuse me, I need to make confession.

PARIS. I was showing the Friar the vows I've written. And I've selected the hymns.

FRIAR LAURENCE. Normally a mass in Latin does not include the "Battle Hymn of the Republic."

PARIS. Where's your patriotism?

FRIAR LAURENCE. Look, don't get married on Thursday.

PARIS. Why?

FRIAR LAURENCE. Why? Why? Why? Why? He wants to know why! *Why?* Juliet'll tell you why.

PARIS. Why?

FRIAR LAURENCE. Hey! You can't talk to the bride before the wedding. That's bad luck according to Jesus. We better cancel Thursday.

PARIS. You'd rather I go to the Methodist minister.

FRIAR LAURENCE. Thursday it is.

PARIS. Juliet, remember your face is mine. Don't slander it with tears.

(He tries to kiss her. She ducks out of the way or coughs grotesquely to dissuade him. He exits. She makes a face and a noise when he's going.)

JULIET. *(mocking PARIS)* Duh, my name's Paris.

FRIAR LAURENCE. Boy, what a jerk. Your face doesn't bel –

JULIET. Shut up! You told him you'd marry us!

FRIAR LAURENCE. I know, I know. What's a Methodist?

JULIET. Focus! I'm already married to Romeo! They still stone women for adultery around here.

FRIAR LAURENCE. It's part of my plan.

JULIET. What's the rest of your plan?

FRIAR LAURENCE. That's as far as I got.

(JULIET pulls out a dagger.)

JULIET. Okay, asshole[31], come up with a solution or I'll kill myself.

FRIAR LAURENCE. Put away that dagger, Juliet. Just let me consult the instruction manual we get from the Pope.

---

31 See Appendix 6 for alternate lyrics and dialogue.

(He takes a book off a shelf downstage and flips through it.)

Okay…yada, yada, yada…"settle out of court,"… Okay, perfect!

(He replaces the book.)

Get married to Paris on Thursday and I'll apply for an annulment. It will only take 8 years.

JULIET. I would rather jump off a tall building into a pit of poisonous snakes and be chewed on by bears and be buried alive with a dead person than marry Paris.

FRIAR LAURENCE. All right, Fear Factor, get on your knees….I've got it…

(On their knees, they're scored by #24 continued, a spare, churchy pad.)

God in heaven, we humbly beseech thee, send Jesus back to earth so He can explain to Juliet's parents why she has two husbands –

JULIET. Get away from me!

(They get up.)

FRIAR LAURENCE. I'm doin' the best I can here, Juliet.

(FRIAR JOHN enters.)

FRIAR LAURENCE. What ho, Friar John.

FRIAR JOHN. Confession's supposed to be a quiet thing. I can hear ya all over the church.

JULIET. I'm better off dead.

FRIAR JOHN. Maybe. *(to FRIAR LAURENCE)* Look, I need some of your special knockout drug. I can never sleep when I go to Mantua.

FRIAR LAURENCE. *(light bulb, see #24)*

Knockout drug, Mantua, this gives me a great idea. Juliet, go home and tell them you will marry Paris on Thursday. Then take this potion on Wednesday night. Now, why I as Catholic priest would have a potion that renders a person temporarily comatose doesn't mean I have an interest in necrophilia. It just means I have a potion around for times like this.

JULIET. Really?

FRIAR LAURENCE. Yes, you would be surprised how many fourteen year old girls need to put themselves in a death-like state to deceive their parents. I think it's an Italian thing. Anyway, drink this, you'll be in stasis for 42 hours.

JULIET. Friar John can take a message to Romeo.

(He types the dictation of "Friar's Letter," #25.)

FRIAR LAURENCE. Right. Take this down. "Dear Romeo, How are you? I am fine. How is the weather in Mantua? What's a Methodist? – "

JULIET. Cut to the chase.

(sings)

THE PRIEST WHO BEARS THIS NOTE IS FRIAR JOHN.

FRIAR LAURENCE.   That's what I'd say.

JULIET.

HIS DISCRETION IS THE KIND YOU CAN RELY ON.

FRIAR LAURENCE.   It's like *I'm* writing.

JULIET.

I GAVE JULIET A VILE LIBATION
THAT PUT HER IN SUSPENDED ANIMATION.

FRIAR JOHN. Like a pie!

JULIET. *(Whatever that means.)* Yes, like a pie. What a curious little man.

FRIAR LAURENCE. You think so, too?

JULIET.

NOW DON'T WORRY, IT IS ONLY TEMPORARY.

FRIAR LAURENCE. That's not for sure.

JULIET. Oh, my God.

(sings)

BUT GET YOUR ASS BACK HERE BEFORE SHE'S BURIED

FRIAR LAURENCE. Don't say ass.

JULIET. *(hits him)*

IN HER FAMILY'S CRYPT KNOWN AS A MAUSOLEUM.

COME GET HER AND TOGETHER YOU CAN FLEE 'EM.

(spoken)

Sign it!

*(He does and crosses to **FRIAR JOHN**.)*

FRIAR LAURENCE.

NOW YOU'RE ON YOUR WAY TO MANTUA

COME HERE, GOOD FRIAR JOHN.

SO LONG, FAREWELL, ADIEU, GOOD LUCK, BE GONE.

FRIAR LAURENCE & JULIET.

SO LONG, FAREWELL, ADIEU, GOOD LUCK, BE GONE.

(Lights change.)

51. INT. DUNGEON[32]

*(The **FRIAR** is seated as before. The **PRINCE** enters, imitating Peter Falk's Columbo.)*

PRINCE. Sir, just one more question, just routine, Sir, I know you're a busy man.

FRIAR LAURENCE. Yes, yes, what is it?

PRINCE. Thank you – this is a huge dungeon, Sir. What do you suppose it costs to heat a room like this?

FRIAR LAURENCE. Did you have a question that pertains to me?

PRINCE. Yes, Sir, bear with me, Sir. This is very confusing, I'm hoping you can clear this up. You gave a fourteen year old girl a speedball. First you marry her, then you gave her a speedball. Isn't that what happened, Sir?

---

32 See Appendix 6 for alternate lyrics and dialogue.

FRIAR LAURENCE. Prince, what the hell are you doing?

PRINCE. Okay, you did the whole *Our Town* thing.

(*The* **PRINCE** *runs off in a hissy huff.*)

52. INT. HALL AT VILLA CAPULET

(**LADY CAPULET** *crosses through with* **GREGORY.** **LORD CAPULET** *enters from elsewhere, taking a snort from a flask.*)

LADY CAPULET. Here's a list. Go to town and invite these people. Oh, and it's in alphabetical order so it's really easy...

CAPULET. What about invitations?

GREGORY. But I can't...

(*He exits.*)

LADY CAPULET. It takes a day to walk to the printer to tell him you want the invitations. The wedding is in two days. Do you ever...

(**JULIET** *enters and curtsies. She lays it on thick.*)

JULIET. Hello, Mama! Hello, Papa! What a glorious Tuesday morning. Forgive me, I was rash before. I am so excited I will marry Paris on Thursday. Well, I'm going out to check on the bridesmaids' dresses.

(**JULIET** *exits skipping.* **LADY CAPULET** *eyes her suspiciously.*)

CAPULET. I knew if I yelled at her she'd see my point of view.

LADY CAPULET. Idiot! She's up to something. Search her room for drugs.

CAPULET. Okay, okay. Let's get her married tomorrow.

LADY CAPULET. Tomorrow? Do you know how long it takes to get ready for a wedding, let alone one that's tomorrow?

CAPULET. Just use the decorations left over from the Fourth of July.

LADY CAPULET. And that's your solution.

CAPULET. I can't believe how difficult you're being.

LADY CAPULET. I can't believe I married you.

CAPULET. What color is my beard?

LADY CAPULET. Red.

CAPULET. What color is your hair?

LADY CAPULET. Blonde.

CAPULET. I can't believe you and I had a brunette daughter.

LADY CAPULET. Why don't you have another drink?

CAPULET. Huzzah! An idea with purpose. Why don't you explain the facts of life to your daughter?

(He exits, drinking. The **NURSE** *enters.)*

LADY CAPULET. Don't worry, I'll tell her. Nurse!

(She reprises the "Trouble" melody in #26, "You've Got to Tell Her.")

YOU'VE GOT TO TELL HER ABOUT HER DUTY[33]
ONCE SHE'S WED AND WEARING PARIS'S RING.
YOU KNOW THE HONEYMOON IN THE BEDROOM.
YOU KNOW THE STUFF ABOUT WHAT'S UP WITH HIS
    THING.

NURSE.

I'M PRETTY SURE JULIET ALREADY KNOWS.

LADY CAPULET.

DOES SHE REALIZE HIS JOHNSON GETS HARD?
YOU BREAST FED HER SO YOU KNOW BETTER.
I JUST SIGN HER REPORT CARD.

NURSE.

NOT ME, YOU TELL HER. I'M JUST A SERVANT,
JUST THE ONE WHO TAKES HER TEMPERATURE!

(From every available entrance, hands clap four times.)

---

33 See Appendix 6 for alternate lyrics and dialogue.

LADY CAPULET.

> YOU MUST ALERT HER, HE'LL PUT HIS THING IN
> TO ANY ONE OF HER THREE APERTURES.
> YOU'VE GOT TO TELL HER.

NURSE.

> NOT ME, YOU TELL HER.

BOTH.

> TELL HER SO SHE'LL KNOW WHAT TO DO!

> *(***LADY CAPULET*** and* **NURSE** *pose and the next musical vamp begins.)*

53. INT. HALL AT VILLA CAPULET – NEXT MORNING

> *(***GREGORY,*** the* **NURSE,** *the* **SERVING WENCH,** *and another* **SERVANT** *prepare the hall for the wedding and attend to the* **CAPULETS** *and* **PARIS** *as everyone sings #27, "It's a Beautiful Day For a Wedding."* **LORD CAPULET** *wears a sash on which the word "Wedding" has crudely replaced "Fourth of July".)*

ALL.

> IT'S A BEAUTIFUL DAY FOR A WEDDING.

CAPULET. *(to another* **SERVANT***)*

> BUT DON'T USE THOSE PEWTER PLATES.

> *(to* **SERVING WENCH***)*

> LET ME HAVE A LOOK AT THE
> PRENUPTIAL AGREEMENT
> FROM PARIS THE CHEAPSKATE.

GREGORY.

> LET ME INTRODUCE THE MUSICIANS.

CAPULET. *(to* **PIANIST** *who stands)*

> I WANT NO COUNTRY MUSIC WITH A TWANG.
> AND UNDER NO CIRCUMSTANCE
> WILL PEOPLE GET UP AND DANCE
> TO THAT SONG BY KOOL AND THE GANG.

ALL.

IT'S A BEAUTIFUL DAY FOR A WEDDING.

CAPULET.

THE TAPESTRY WILL COVER UP THAT FURNITURE.

(The **SERVANT** *puts a "Don't Tread on Me" flag on the bench left.)*

LADY CAPULET.

I'M REMINDED OF MY WEDDING TO THE LORD
CAPULET.

CAPULET & LADY CAPULET.

IT WAS ALSO HELL IN MIN'ATURE.

ALL.

IT'S SUCH A BEAUTIFUL DAY FOR A WEDDING.

(The **SERVANT** *gives* **CAPULET** *a bottle.)*

CAPULET.

ALCOHOL'S THE CURE.

(All continue wedding preparation activities in rhythm as lights change...)

54. INT. MOTEL MANTUA/INT. VILLA CAPULET

(...to the Mantua special featuring **ROMEO** *as he enters.)*

ROMEO.

I'VE BEEN IN MOTEL MANTUA
A TOTAL OF TWELVE HOURS.
IT'S DREARY AND IT'S DIRTY SO I
HAD TO TAKE THREE SHOWERS,
THE MOST EXCITING THING I'VE DONE.
MY BANISHMENT IS CRUEL,
LIKE LISTENING TO A HOCKEY FAN
EXPLAIN THE ICING RULE.

(The rest of the cast supplies background vocals and sways with a partner: **GREGORY** *with* **SAMPSON,** **CAPULET** *with* **ANOTHER SERVANT, PARIS** *with the* **SERVING WENCH,** *and the* **NURSE** *with* **LADY CAPULET**.*)*

I'M JONESIN' FOR JULIET.
MY SHIP SEEKS HER PORT.
ASSIGN JUSTICE JULIET
TO ROMEO'S COURT.
I'LL WORK ON MY METAPHORS
BUT MANTUA'S A BLOODY BORE
IT'S WORSE THAN ANY TIME YOU SPENT
WITH FRIAR IN SUNDAY SCHOOL.

*(***ROMEO*** exits when lights bump up.)*

55. INT. HALL AT VILLA CAPULET/INT. JULIET'S CHAMBER

*(***JULIET*** enters her chamber.)*

ALL.

IT'S A BEAUTIFUL DAY FOR A WEDDING.

*(***GREGORY*** arrives with flowers.)*

CAPULET.

PUT THOSE FLOWERS OVER THERE.

PARIS. *(to* **CAPULET***)*

I'D LIKE TO KISS MY JULIET
ONE TIME BEFORE I WED HER.

*(***LADY CAPULET*** gives **JULIET** the book "Faking It.")*

LADY CAPULET.

READ THIS BOOK AND BE PREPARED.

PARIS.

HERE'S A COPY OF THE SERVICE.

CAPULET.

> STICK TO THE SCRIPT AND BE PROFOUND.
> NO AD LIBS OR IMPRO
> BECAUSE THE NEXT THING YOU KNOW
> YOU'RE DOING
>
> *(**CAPULET**, **PARIS**, **GREGORY** and **SERVANT** form a jocular barbershop quartet for 2 bars.)*

CAPULET, PARIS, GREGORY & SERVANT.

> SCENES STRAIGHT FROM *OUR TOWN.*

CAPULET.

> IT'S A

ALL.

> BEAUTIFUL DAY FOR A WEDDING.
>
> *(**GREGORY** returns with flowers.)*

CAPULET.

> GOD DAMN IT PUT THOSE FLOWERS OVER THERE.[34]
>
> *(He throws them.)*

LADY CAPULET.

> I'M REMINDED OF THE REASON WE SLEEP IN
> SEPARATE BEDS.

CAPULET.

> AM I THE ONLY ONE 'ROUND HERE WHO CARES?
>
> *(They give each other the finger.)*

ALL.

> IT'S A BEAUTIFUL DAY FOR A WEDDING.
> LOVE IS IN THE AIR.
>
> *(The cast continues moving in rhythm as lights change and...)*

56. INT. JULIET'S CHAMBER/INT. HALL AT VILLA CAPULET

*(**JULIET** sings her obligado.)*

---

[34] See Appendix 6 for alternate lyrics and dialogue.

JULIET.
> FRIAR, LET YOUR POTION
> DO ITS MAGIC STUFF.
> HERE'S TO ROMEO, MY LOVE,
> I HOPE I'VE GOT ENOUGH.
>
> *(She drinks. Lights bump up.)*

57. INT. HALL/EXT. MANTUA/INT. JULIET'S CHAMBER

> *(The cast reprises choreography from the opening number.)*

ALL.
> IT'S A BEAUTIFUL DAY FOR A WEDDING.

ROMEO.
> THIS EXILE IS NOT MEANT FOR NORMAL MAN.

JULIET.
> IF THE POTION DOESN'T WORK, I COULD ALWAYS
> JOIN THE CIRCUS.
>
> *(**GREGORY** still has flowers.)*

CAPULET.
> PUT THE FLOWERS OVER THERE! GOD DAMN![35]
>
> *(**CAPULET** throws flowers again.)*

ALL.
> IT'S A BEAUTIFUL,

ROMEO.
> MIS'RABLE,

JULIET.
> CHEMICAL

ALL.
> DAY FOR A WEDDING,
> IF EVERYTHING GOES AS PLANNED!
>
> *(All except **JULIET** run off. Music segues to #28 immediately.)*

---

[35] See Appendix 6 for alternate lyrics and dialogue.

58. INT. JULIET'S CHAMBER

(The **NURSE** *and* **GREGORY**, *who carries flowers, enter.* **JULIET** *lies unconscious. The* **NURSE** *cannot awaken* **JULIET**. *She sings #28, "Woe.")*

NURSE. Get up, sleepyhead, it's your wedding day! What's this? Juliet is dead! Oh, no! Oh, woe!

(singing)

O WOE! O WOE! O WOEFUL DAY
THAT I E'ER DID YET BEHOLD.
O DAY ,O DAY, O HATEFUL DAY!
JULIET IS DEAD AND COLD.
O WOE, O DREADFUL FUCKING WOE.[36]
THIS GIRL MORE PRECIOUS THAN GOLD.
HOW WILL I FIND ANOTHER JOB?
I'M FIFTY FOUR YEARS OLD.
O WOE O WOE O WOE O WOE
OH BLA DI BLA DA.

*(***LADY CAPULET*** enters.)*

LADY CAPULET. What is going on here?

GREGORY. Juliet is dead, and Nurse is upset because she's gonna lose her job.

LADY CAPULET.

ACCURSED, UNHAPPY, WRETCHED DAY.
O ME, MY CHILD, MY LIFE!
THIS LITTLE GIRL, THE FRUIT OF MY WOMB,
THE REASON I'M CAPULET'S WIFE.
DEATH HAS CATCHED YOU FROM MY SIGHT
AND WITH YOU FLEES MY LORD.
HE'LL FIND SOMEONE YOUNGER, I'M SURE OF IT.
I'M A WORN OUT OVERPRICED WHORE!
O ME, O ME, O ME, ME O.
EENIE MEENIE MINIE MO.

NURSE. Come here, Phyllis.

---

[36] See Appendix 6 for alternate lyrics and dialogue.

(They hug each other and wail. **LORD CAPULET**
enters.)

CAPULET. Okay, the Friar's not here yet, but let's get
this show on the road…what is going on here?

GREGORY. Juliet is dead, the Nurse is upset about
losing her job, and m'Lady is pretty much saying
what she always says.

CAPULET.

O NO, SHE IS DEFLOWER'D BY DEATH.
THE WEDDING'S NOW A WAKE.
IT'S EASY ENOUGH TO FIRE THE BAND
BUT WHAT'LL I DO WITH THE CAKE?

LADY CAPULET. The cake!

CAPULET.

O WOE O WOE AY YI YI YI,
NA NA NA, HEY HEY HEY GOODBYE

(Trio. The nonsense syllables form a mournful cat-
erwauling.)

NURSE.

OH BLA,

LADY CAPULET.

ME O,

CAPULET.

SHA NA NA NA.

ALL THREE.

O WOE WOE O WOE WOE O WOE.
SHA NA, DE BLA, ME O, ME O,
E I E I O.

*(***PARIS** *enters.)*

PARIS. One of the bridesmaids just…What is going on
here?

GREGORY. Dead, no job, whore, and…

(sings)

OL' MACDONALD HAD A FARM.

PARIS.

> BEGUILED, DIVORCED, SPITED, AND SLAIN!
> BY DEATH I HAVE BEEN WRONGED.
> GET UP, GIRL, I PAID FOR THIS
> AND WAITED TOO DAMN LONG.

CAPULET.

> PARIS, STAY AS LONG AS YOU NEED.

PARIS.

> YES, THAT WOULD BE WONDERFUL.

> *(He exits, crying.)*

CAPULET & LADY CAPULET.

> IT'S THE LEAST WE CAN DO CONSIDERING
> THE DOWRY'S NONREFUNDABLE.

> *(The lights change.)*

59. INT. DUNGEON

*(**PRINCE** and **FRIAR**. The **CAPULETS** remain in tableau.)*

PRINCE. Why were you late? You could have prevented Juliet from taking the potion.

FRIAR LAURENCE. Nobody told me the ceremony had been moved up a day.

PRINCE. Oh, for cryin' out loud! It was a ceremony you were performing.

> *(The **PRINCE** shoves **FRIAR** into the flashback.)*

60. INT. JULIET'S CHAMBER

*(**LORD CAPULET, LADY CAPULET,** and **GREGORY** still mourn **JULIET**'s apparent demise. The **FRIAR** enters.)*

FRIAR LAURENCE. Hey, what's this? Juliet is dead? Wow, this is really sad. Well, you have no recourse but to let her body lie in state unguarded in the mausoleum as is our custom.

(He smiles.)

CAPULET. Gregory, go to the houses of all the guests and tell them it's not a wedding. It's a funeral.... and put those motherfucking flowers over there![37]

(He grabs the flowers and throws them. All exit as lights change.)

61. INT. A MOTEL IN MANTUA

(BENVOLIO runs up to ROMEO.)

ROMEO. Benvolio, what news from Verona?

BENVOLIO. Well, I've got good news. You're free to...

(BENVOLIO sings #29, a reprise of "See Other People.")

SEE OTHER PEOPLE
'CAUSE JULIET'S DEAD!
BECAUSE YOU WERE BANISHED
SHE WENT OFF HER HEAD.

ROMEO. How is that good news?

BENVOLIO. I guess it's not.

(ROMEO sings #30, "The Score.")

ROMEO.
JULIET, I'LL FIND A WAY
TO LIE WITH THEE TONIGHT.
MY BANISHMENT IS DONE.

BENVOLIO.
I'LL SIGN YOU OUT.

(BENVOLIO exits. ROMEO moves up center.)

---

37 See Appendix 6 for alternate lyrics and dialogue.

62. EXT. MANTUA/INT. SEEDY STOREFRONT

(The song does not break stride.)

ROMEO.

AND I'LL TAKE FLIGHT.
LUCKILY THE SKID ROW PART
OF MANTUA IS SCARY.
WHAT HO! APOTHECARY!

*(The **APOTHECARY**, who is something out of an 80s hair band, enters.)*

APOTHECARY.

WHO'S THERE?

ROMEO.

ROMEO.

APOTHECARY.

MY NAME IS GARY.

*(They shake hands and go inside the **APOTHE-CARY'S** domain. Two **ASSISTANT APOTHECARIES** AKA **GARY'S GIRLS** enter and dance like go-go girls and provide back up vocals.)*

ROMEO.

GARY, I NEED POISON.

APOTHECARY.

I GOT ARSENIC AND MORPHINE,
HEROIN AND HASHISH
AND METHAMPHETAMINES.
WHAT IS THE OCCASION?

ROMEO.

IT IS MY SUICIDE.

APOTHECARY.

THEN YOU'LL WANT CYANIDE.

ROMEO.

IN CONVENIENT LIQUID FORM.

APOTHECARY.

MY POVERTY BUT NOT MY WILL CONSENTS.

ROMEO.

GIMME THE POISON AND SAVE YOUR ELOQUENCE.

APOTHECARY. Take it with food or it's too intense!

(He gives **ROMEO** *the poison.)*

THAT'LL BE THIRTY DUCATS.

ROMEO.

HERE'S FORTY, KEEP THE CHANGE.

MONEY IS MORE MURDEROUS

THAN ANY POISON YOU HAVE ARRANGED.

APOTHECARY.

HERE'S A COUPON FOR THE NEXT TIME.

THANK YOU, COME AGAIN.

PLEASE TELL ALL YOUR FRIENDS.

(spoken)

I mean, I'm dying in this location.

ASSISTANT APOTHECARIES.

TELL ALL YOUR FRIENDS.

(The **APOTHECARY** *exits. His assistants remain and provide b.g. vocals as the scene transforms and...)*

63. INT. FRIAR LAURENCE'S CELL

("The Score" continues. **FRIAR LAURENCE** *receives* **FRIAR JOHN.***)*

FRIAR LAURENCE. What ho, Friar John?

FRIAR JOHN.

I COULDN'T GET YOUR LETTER THROUGH.

THE TOWN WAS QUARANTINED.

FRIAR LAURENCE.

THEN YOU FLASH YOUR FUCKIN' CLERGY BADGE.

IT GETS YOU INTO ANY SCENE.[38]

FRIAR JOHN.

I TOOK IT OFF TO SHOW IT TO A NUN JUST TO IMPRESS HER

THEN I LEFT IT AT HOME ON MY DRESSER.

---

38 See Appendix 6 for alternate lyrics and dialogue.

FRIAR LAURENCE.

YOU LEFT YOUR BADGE ON YOUR DRESSER TO
IMPRESS HER.

(As **ASSISTANT APOTHECARIES** *trade ab libs,
vamp continues under furious* **FRIAR LAURENCE**.*)*

You know what this means, Friar John! Scandal!
Ruin! Prison! One of us is going to jail, and it's not
gonna be me!

(sings again)

YOU'RE FRIAR JOHN THE BAPTIST.

FRIAR JOHN.

WHY DO YOU CALL ME THAT?

FRIAR LAURENCE.

'CAUSE I WANT YOUR HEAD ON A PLATTER,
YOU BRAINLESS SACK OF FAT.

(He throws **FRIAR JOHN** *off)*

JULIET WAITS AT THE TOMB,
AND THEREBY HANGS A TALE.

(And the scene transforms…)

64. INT. DUNGEON

(The **PRINCE** *enters and speaks in rhythm. Again the
two backup singers ad lib twos. In the dialogue, change
"Skokie Swift" to something that makes sense locally. In
L.A., for instance, use the phrase "surface streets.")*

PRINCE. But it's you who's here in jail. You know,
there's no record of a quarantine.

FRIAR. I'm telling you there was.

PRINCE. Then how did Benvolio get to Mantua?

FRIAR. I don't know. Maybe he took the Skokie Swift.
All I'm telling you is what Friar John told me.

PRINCE.

WHO DO YOU THINK YOU'RE DEALING WITH?

THERE IS NO OTHER FRIAR.

ASSISTANT APOTHECARIES.

NO, NO, NO!

FRIAR LAURENCE.

HE TRANSFERRED HERE FROM VENICE!

PRINCE.

MY PATIENCE HAS EXPIRED.

YOU CREATED HIM AND I DON'T BUY YOUR ALIBI,

SO GOODBYE,

PRINCE & THE ASSISTANT APOTHECARIES.

IT'S TIME FOR YOU TO DIE.

PRINCE.

MAY GOD FORGIVE YOU ALL YOUR LIES.

(All exit but **FRIAR LAURENCE**, *who sings #31, "Friar's Prayer.")*

FRIAR LAURENCE.

MAYBE IT'S PURELY COINCIDENCE[39]

OR A SERIES OF RANDOM EVENTS

BUT THE SHIT HIT THE FAN

AND GUESS WHO'S THE FAN.

I'M DOOMED BUT I'M INNOCENT.

FRIAR LAURENCE. *(cont.)*

THE PRINCE IS MERELY DOING HIS JOB

AND DOING IT WELL, I'LL CONCEDE HIM.

BUT I'VE BEEN A PRIEST FOR LIKE 25 YEARS

SO WHERE IS MY GOD WHEN I NEED HIM?

(Tempo 2)

GOD, YOU'RE A GRACIOUS GOD,

BUT PLEASE REVISE YOUR DECISION

TO HAVE ME KILLED AND BEFORE I FORGET

WHY'D YOU INVENT CIRCUMCISION?

GOD, THEY SAY THAT YOU ARE LOVE

BUT THERE'S ALL OF THIS BLOODSHED AND PAIN.

---

[39] See Appendix 6 for alternate lyrics and dialogue.

GOD, YOU'RE A FICKLE GOD,
AND I'M NOT THE FIRST TO COMPLAIN.

(Tempo 1)

YOU'RE GREAT, YOU'RE HOLY, I SERVED YOU WELL
MY WHOLE LIFE AND NEVER GAVE UP.
SO I DIDN'T PRAY FOR A COUPLE OF DAYS.
YOU WOULD THINK I'D HAVE CREDIT SAVED UP.
NOW IF YOU'RE OMNISCIENT – NOW DON'T GET UPSET –
I ASK WHY SHOULD WE PRAY IN THE FIRST PLACE?
IF YOU READ MINDS, SAVE US ALL TIME,
TELL US WHEN WE FALL FROM GRACE!

(Tempo 2)

GOD, YOU MADE DINOSAURS
THEN KILLED THEM ALL WITH AN ICE FLOE,
OR AN ASTEROID OR SOMETHING ELSE.
THE POINT IS: WHAT YOU SAY, IT GOES.
GOD, ABOVE ALL ELSE,
IT'S YOUR NAME I REVERENTLY HALLOW.
GOD, DOUBLE CHECK YOUR PLAN
'CAUSE I'M ON MY WAY TO THE GALLOWS.
I'VE GOT PLENTY OF OPTIONS.
IF YOU LET ME DOWN,
I'LL GO WORSHIP THE BIRD-GOD OSIRIS!
SURE, YOU MADE PLANTS AND ROCKS AND SEAS
BUT HE INVENTED PAPYRUS.
OR I'LL SPREAD THE WORD WE'RE DESCENDED FROM
    APES
'CAUSE EVOLUTION DEFAMES THEE.
OK, GOD, I WAS BLUFFING THEN BUT COME ON!
CAN YOU REALLY BLAME ME?

(Lights change. There are **8 BACKGROUND VOCAL-ISTS** *gathered around the piano.)*

GOD, YOU GAVE US YOUR SON,
AND THAT WHOLE EASTER STORY STILL GRABS US.
REMEMBER ME BACK IN SUNDAY SCHOOL,
I PLAYED THE PART OF BARABBAS.
GOD, IF YOU LET ME LIVE,

I WON'T DARKEN INIQUITY'S DOOR.
GOD, THIS IS LARRY, GOD.
I'LL NEVER DO WRONG ANYMORE!

(Blackout.)

65. INT. THE TOMB

(Lights up. **ROMEO** *arrives and sees* **JULIET** *lying in state.)*

ROMEO. Juliet, you can't possibly be dead, you're so good looking...maybe you're not...yes, maybe you're in a coma...yes, you could wake up any second....Oh, you're dead, who the hell am I kidding?

(He does a ventriloquist bit with the lifeless **JULIET***.)*

"Don't cry, Romeo, I'm not dead. I love you. I am happy and singing. I wanna make out more."

(He weeps.)

What the hell am I doing?

*(***PARIS** *enters.)*

PARIS. What the hell are you doing, freak show?

ROMEO. I happen to be mourning my wife.

PARIS. *Your* wife!?

(He sings #32, "I'm Going to Kill You.")

I'M GOING TO KILL YOU!

ROMEO.   Oh, geez.

PARIS.

I BELIEVE IT'S GOD'S WILL TO.
YOU KILLED TYBALT. SHE CONTRACTED FATAL GRIEF.

ROMEO.

LOOK, DON'T EVEN PUSH ME.
I HAPPEN TO LOVE HER.

PARIS.

> YOU INSULT ME WHEN YOU LIE LIKE SOME SMALL
> THIEF.
> YOU WOULD DEFILE HER GRAVE,
> YOU NECROPHILIATIC KNAVE.
> FEEL MY SWORD EXPRESS THE METTLE OF MY HATE!
> I'M GOING TO KILL Y –

ROMEO. *(stabbing* **PARIS***)*

> TOO LATE!

PARIS. You call that a stab?[40]

> *(***ROMEO*** throws a dagger at him. ***PARIS*** makes an
> SFX so we know it hits the mark.)*
>
> Oh, boy I hope I don't fall on that. Oh shit, oh
> shit.
>
> *(***PARIS*** falls on the dagger and dies. ***ROMEO*** sings
> #33, "Thank You for Dying First.")*

ROMEO.

> AH, DEAR JULIET,
> WHY ART THOUGH SO FAIR?
> THOSE FOLKS AT THE FUNERAL HOME
> DID WONDERS WITH YOUR HAIR.
> NOW I'LL MOURN YOU IN MONOLOGUE
> 'CAUSE I'M A GREAT BIG STAGE HOG!
> THANK YOU FOR DYING FIRST!
>
> *(verse)*
>
> I KNOW THERE ARE OPTIONS
> TO THIS SUICIDE SENTENCE.
> PERHAPS YOUR EMBALMER
> COULD USE AN APPRENTICE.
> BUT GRIEF IS SO PRIMITIVE,
> MY THINKING IS LIMITED.
> THANK YOU FOR DYING FIRST!
>
> *(During the bridge,* **ROMEO** *picks up the "Don't
> Tread on Me" flag and dances with it on the bench
> left. He then covers* **PARIS**' *body with the flag.)*

---

40 See Appendix 6 for alternate lyrics and dialogue.

IF I WENT FIRST WITHOUT A TRACE,
YOU'D BE WED TO THAT MAN'S FACE.
SORRY YOU EVER MET THAT TWIT.
YOUR DEATH HAS GOT SOME MERIT
IN THAT PARIS WON'T INHERIT
ALL MY LIFE INSURANCE BENEFITS.

(verse)

I THINK THAT I'LL DRINK THIS BEFORE
SOMEONE GETS IN
PLUS I'D RATHER NOT SEE YOUR RIGOR
MORTIS SET IN.
THOUGH I'M SAD MY BABY'S GONE,
MY SPEECH WAS A WHOLE PAGE LONG.
THANKS, HERE'S MUD IN YOUR EYE.

(7 "glugs" in rhythm, kiss on 8)

THUS WITH A KISS I DIE.
THANK YOU FOR DYING...
I'M FEELING NOTHING.

(He crawls like Jolson)

THANK YOU FOR DYING–

(Spoken, as it suddenly hits him)

Damn, Gary, this is strong shit.[41]

(He collapses)

–FIRST.

*(**ROMEO** dies. Blackout. Note: in the dark, the assistant stage manager, wearing a duplicate suit and "Don't Tread on Me" flag, takes the place of **PARIS** on the floor.)*

---

41 See Appendix 6 for alternate lyrics and dialogue.

66. INT./EXT VILLA CAPULET

(Lights up. **LORD CAPULET** *stands with a* **WOMAN IN THE AUDIENCE.***)*

CAPULET. You know, you're one of the best serving wenches we've got around here…. My wife doesn't understand me.

(Lights change.)

67. INT. THE TOMB – SECONDS AFTER ROMEO'S DEATH

(The bodies of **ROMEO**, **JULIET**, *and* **PARIS** *litter the stage.* **FRIAR LAURENCE** *enters.)*

FRIAR LAURENCE. Hello? Hello? Is someone in the mausoleum… (sees **ROMEO**) What the fuck! Romeo! How the hell did you get here so fast? I live next door! You came all the way from Mantua! What do I pay that security company for?[42]

(sees **PARIS***)*

Double what the fuck!

*(*JULIET *wakes up.)*

JULIET. Oh comfortable Friar!

FRIAR LAURENCE. Triple what the fuck! I knew that was coming and still! Yes, Juliet, it is I, the comfort-giving but currently uncomfortable Friar Laurence.

JULIET. Where is my lord? I do remember where I should be, and there I am. Where is my Romeo?

FRIAR LAURENCE. Juliet, I have good news and bad news and good news.

JULIET. What is the bad news?

FRIAR LAURENCE. The bad news, honey, is that Romeo is dead. See for yourself, he's right down there. But the good news is that Paris is also dead.

---

[42] See Appendix 6 for alternate lyrics and dialogue.

JULIET. Two dead husbands?

FRIAR LAURENCE. Yeah, now don't focus on the negative.

JULIET. What's the other good news?

FRIAR LAURENCE. The other good news...You're free to

(sings #34)

SEE OTHER PEOPLE, BY THAT I MEAN DATE –

JULIET. Cut it out.

(knocking offstage, done by **MAN 2** *or* **3***)*

FRIAR LAURENCE. The mausoleum is closed! Look at it this way, Juliet. Romeo is dead, okay, that's a drag, but Paris is also dead, and those deaths kinda cancel each other out. Find another husband. Third time's a charm.

JULIET. Why don't you try a knock-knock joke while you're at it?

FRIAR LAURENCE. Knock-knock.

JULIET. Cut it out.

(two knocks offstage)

FRIAR LAURENCE. Who's there? All right, I guess someone wants to tour the mausoleum or something. It happens. Here, look at this convent brochure. I'm going to take you there forthwith.

(More offstage knocking)

I'm coming! These are not normal mausoleum hours!

(The scene transforms, scored by the A minor figure in #34.)

68. INT. DUNGEON

(The **FRIAR** *paces and then admits an* **EXECU-TIONER**, *a middle-aged woman who probably knitted the sweater she's wearing.)*

EXECUTIONER. Friar Laurence?

FRIAR LAURENCE. Yes.

EXECUTIONER. Hi there, I'm Terry. I'm gonna be your executioner. This won't take a minute and then we'll get you out to the gallows.

FRIAR LAURENCE. I thought it was the electric chair.

EXECUTIONER. My work order says "death by hanging."

FRIAR LAURENCE. Great, that'll be better.

EXECUTIONER. Me and the guys at the shop get a kick out of you...leaving a confused teenager alone with her dead lover and a sword.

FRIAR LAURENCE. I didn't know what she was gonna do!

EXECUTIONER. What did you think she was gonna do? A crossword puzzle? She threatened to kill herself a couple of days before.

FRIAR LAURENCE. That was different! Romeo was banished.

(From somewhere, **ROMEO** *bawls at "banished.")*

EXECUTIONER. So now he was dead, so it was worse.

FRIAR LAURENCE. Well, I wish you'da been there.

EXECUTIONER. You never should have left that mausoleum.

(Lights return focus to the tomb.)

69. INT. THE TOMB

*(*JULIET *cradles* **ROMEO***'s head.)*

JULIET. *(ventriloquist bit)* Do you mean that, Romeo?

"Why, yes I do, Juliet. You were always the better kisser. I'm so sorry I only learned how to kiss a day before I died. Kind of ironic."

(She lets him flop to floor. She sings #35, her reprise of "Thank You for Dying First.")

JULIET. *(sings)*
POISON, I SEE, HAS BEEN
MY TRUE LOVE'S TIMELESS END.
YOUR BODY STILL IS WARM
AND I WON'T DARE PRETEND
SINCE I'M AN INGENUE
THE SCENERY'S ALL MINE TO CHEW.
THANK YOU FOR DYING FIRST.
I KNOW THAT YOU WERE HEAVEN SENT.
AND THE FIFTEEN HOURS THAT WE SPENT
WERE MAGICAL AND NEW TO ME.
GLAD TO SEE YOU HAVE MY RING
AND MAN, YOU SAID SOME FUNNY THINGS.

*(***BARNEY*** *and the* ***NURSE*** *come on from their scene 30 entrances.)*

DON'T EVEN THINK OF INTERRUPTING.

*(***BARNEY*** *and the* ***NURSE*** *exit sheepishly and immediately.)*

JULIET. *(cont.)*
IS THIS A DAGGER
THAT I SEE BEFORE ME?
LIKE A BULL'S HORN,
I BET, IT'S GONNA GORE ME.
YES, I AM A DRAMA QUEEN
EXITING MY BIG SCENE.
THANK YOU FOR DYING FIRST.

(She dies next to him. He comes back to life.)

ROMEO.
GARY, THIS DOPE IS SO
LIKE SMOKING OREGANO!

THANK YOU FOR DYING FIRST.

(He dies. She is revived.)

JULIET.

GEE, DID THAT REALLY SMART
BUT SOMEHOW I MISSED MY HEART.
THANK YOU FOR DYING FIRST.

(She dies. Then they both spring to life.)

BOTH.

MY GOD, YOU'RE STILL ALIVE.
I CAN'T BELIEVE MY EYES.
FRIAR, COME HURRY BACK.
BRING SYRUP OF IPECAC!
WE HAVE BOTH DODGED A CURSE.
SUDDENLY I FEEL WORSE.
GO AHEAD, YOU DIE...

ROMEO.

I'M FEELING NAUSEOUS.

BOTH.

GO AHEAD, YOU DIE...

JULIET.

NO, AFTER YOU, DEAR.

BOTH.

GO AHEAD, YOU DIE...
TALK ABOUT BAD TIMING!
GO AHEAD, YOU DIE...FIRST!

(As they hold the last note, they upstage one another. Then they die. **FRIAR** *returns.)*

FRIAR LAURENCE. Anybody want a copy of *The Watchtower*?

(He tosses it aside.)

Aw, Juliet, I was gone for like 2 minutes.

*(**GREGORY** enters with flowers.)*

GREGORY. Friar Laurence, what is going on here?

FRIAR LAURENCE. Gregory! Boy am I glad to see you.

GREGORY. Stay right where you are, Friar.

(**CAPULET** *enters.*)

CAPULET. What is going on here?

(**GREGORY** *throws the flowers so* **CAPULET** *doesn't see.*)

GREGORY. It look likes Friar Laurence killed Romeo and Paris.

CAPULET. And Juliet. I found this vial labeled "Friar Laurence's Special Knockout Drug" in her room.

(**LADY CAPULET** *enters.*)

LADY CAPULET. What's going on here?

GREGORY. It looks like Friar Laurence killed Romeo and Juliet and Paris.

LADY CAPULET. And he's responsible for the death of the Nurse. She was so distraught over Juliet's death she killed herself.

FRIAR LAURENCE. Thank God. Because if she came through that door right now I'd *really* freak out.

(**MONTAGUE** *enters.*)

MONTAGUE. What is going on here?

ALL. Lord Montague!

GREGORY. Friar Laurence is responsible for at least four deaths.

MONTAGUE. Try seven. Romeo's mother has killed herself and Rosencrantz and Guildenstern are dead.

FRIAR LAURENCE. People, people, there are other ways to deal with adversity besides suicide!

(*The* **PRINCE** *enters.*)

PRINCE. What is going on here?

ALL. Prince Escalus!

FRIAR LAURENCE. Christ! I can't get a letter delivered, but news of "trouble at the tomb" is across town in five seconds!

(Everyone talks to the **PRINCE** *at once.* **CAPULET** *produces Leonard the stuffed animal.)*

CAPULET. ...this bear is an orphan because of him!

PRINCE. Ah, I see. The Friar is responsible for the deaths of 18...

*(***GREGORY*** slices open his own belly and collapses. See Appendix 3.)*

PRINCE. *(cont.)* – rack 'em up, 19 people and the destabilization of our democratic way of life.

FRIAR LAURENCE. Wait a minute, this isn't a democracy!

CAPULET. Yeah, thanks to you, Friar!

PRINCE. All right, that's it...You two: make up.

MONTAGUE. Brother Capulet, we've been doomed from the beginning.

CAPULET. Next time, let's listen more carefully to the opening number.

(FX: FLASH! —A grip-and-grin photograph is taken.)

PRINCE. Thank you, DaVinci, we'll need 5 by 7's for everybody. For never was a story of more woe than this of Juliet and her Romeo.

(Everyone nods meaningfully.)

ALL. Hmm.

PRINCE. Okay, I need statements from everybody.

(Everyone talks at once. Blackout.)

70. INT. DUNGEON

(Lights up. **TERRY THE EXECUTIONER** *picks up where she left off.)*

EXECUTIONER. You never should have left that mausoleum.

FRIAR LAURENCE. I heard you the first time.

(The **PRINCE** *enters with some documents.)*

PRINCE. Friar, sign here….and here….and here.

FRIAR LAURENCE. What am I signing?

PRINCE. That is your confession.

FRIAR LAURENCE. This is not my handwriting.

PRINCE. They're not your words either. Ha, ha. Nice work on the gallows, Terry.

EXECUTIONER. Thank you. It should be a slow and painful death.

PRINCE. Great, people love that. You ready for the big day?

FRIAR LAURENCE. *(sarcastically)* Yeah, I'm really excited about it.

PRINCE. Hey, mister, don't you ruin this for everyone else.

(The **PRINCE** *exits.)*

EXECUTIONER. I have some interesting news for you.

(The **EXECUTIONER** *removes a mask. #36 scores mask removal.)*

FRIAR LAURENCE. Benvolio! That's a *(sings)* FANTAS-TIC MASK!

BENVOLIO. Yeah, isn't it.

FRIAR LAURENCE. You've come to set me free.

BENVOLIO. I've come to show you the face of your executioner.

(He removes another mask.)

FRIAR LAURENCE. Friar John! You curious son of a bitch! You set me up so you could get my job.

FRIAR JOHN. Close.

(He removes yet another mask…and lets down her hair.)

FRIAR LAURENCE. Rosaline!

ROSALINE. That's right.

FRIAR LAURENCE. I know this has been said before but those masks are fucking fantastic.[43]

ROSALINE. The only hard part was getting a copy of *The Watchtower.* Romeo fooled around on me. When I came to you for comfort you took advantage of me.

(She slaps him.)

And then you told Romeo I wasn't worth it. Now I've been in a convent and the nuns are all over me.

FRIAR LAURENCE. So that's why you set me up!

ROSALINE. That's right, asshole.[44]

PRINCE. *(offstage)* I don't know, I'll check with Terry.

(The **FRIAR** *runs to the door and urgently ushers in the* **PRINCE.** **ROSALINE** *puts the masks back on in quick succession.)*

PRINCE. Slow down. Everything okay here, Terry?

FRIAR LAURENCE. That's not Terry.

ROSALINE. Yes, Prince.

FRIAR LAURENCE. I have new information in my defense!

PRINCE. I have a confession, signed by you.

FRIAR LAURENCE. That's not Terry. That's Rosaline.

PRINCE. Right, and I'm Paris. Come on. This is going to the best show ever.

(The **CAPULETS, SAMPSON, LORD MONTAGUE, GREGORY,** *and* **ANOTHER GUY** *comprise a mob and enter noisily as lights change and #36 continues.)*

43, 44 See Appendix 6 for alternate lyrics and dialogue.

71. EXT. THE GALLOWS

(**TERRY/ROSALINE** *drags the* **FRIAR** *to the gallows stage right with the help of the mob. FX: A noose flies in. With the rope around his neck, the* **FRIAR** *finishes #36, a reprise of his "Prayer." The mob freezes.*)

FRIAR LAURENCE.

GOD, IN SPITE OF EVERYTHING,
I STILL SUPPORT INQUISITIONS.
I FAVOR MORE MIDDLE EASTERN CRUSADES AND
MORE FILMS LIKE THAT ONE BY MEL GIBSON.
GOD, YOUR FORGIVENESS, GOD,
IS IT CARTE BLANCHE, OR DOES IT DEPEND?
CAN WE REPENT ALL WHEN WE DIE?
CAN WE JUST DICK AROUND 'TIL THE END?[45]

(The lights come up full. The mob yells.)

Hey, look everybody, here comes God!

(**GOD**, *played by the actor who plays the* **PRINCE**, *arrives in a* Deus Ex Machina, *meaning he walks down the stairs through the audience or glides on astride a razor scooter. Everyone sings #37, "Hallelujah," the finale.*)

CHORUS.

HALLELUJAH, HIP HOORAY, WELL WHADDAYA KNOW!
GOD HAS APPEARED TO WRAP THINGS UP IN ONE
NICE BOW.

(**GOD** *plays a trombone fanfare. Note: any brass or reed instrument will do. Change the "trombone" lyric accordingly.*)

GOD.

YES, I AM GOD.

FRIAR.

SO YOUR TROMBONE ANNOUNCED.

---

45 See Appendix 6 for alternate lyrics and dialogue.

GOD.

> IN A *DEUS EX MACHINA*
> OR HOWEVER THAT'S PRONOUNCED.

FRIAR LAURENCE.

> YOU LOOK LIKE THE PRINCE.

GOD.

> I CHOSE HIS HUMAN FORM.
> IT WAS EITHER HIM OR GEORGE WENDT,
> THE GUY FROM *CHEERS!* NAMED NORM.

CHORUS.   Norm!

> HALLELUJAH, HOLY SMOKE, GREAT BALLS OF FIRE!
> GOD, PLEASE HAVE MERCY, BUT WE GOTTA KILL THE
>   FRIAR.

LADY CAPULET.

> HE KILLED MY DAUGHTER.

GOD.

> NOW PUT AWAY THAT ROPE

> *(The rope disappears to the amazement of all.)*

> ACCORDING TO THE BIBLE,

CHORUS.

> (A LOT OF WHICH HE WROTE)

GOD.

> YES, I DO DECLARE, THE FRIAR IS SET FREE.

> *(The* **FRIAR** *jumps off the gallows.)*

LADY CAPULET.

> WHERE IS THAT WRITTEN?

GOD.

> GALOSHES, CHAPTER THREE.

CHORUS.

> HALLELUJAH, HI DE HI DE HI DE HO!

FRIAR LAURENCE.

> GOD, PLEASE REVIVE JULIET AND ROMEO.

GOD.

> BUT I'D HAVE TO BRING BACK MERCUTIO AND
> EVERYONE WHO'S EVER BEEN ALIVE.

LADY CAPULET.

SHOW ME, GOD, WHERE IS THAT WRITTEN?

GOD.

FALLOPIANS, CHAPTER FIVE.

TRUST ME, FRIAR, THIS TOO SHALL PASS.

FRIAR LAURENCE.

BUT THEY DIED BEFORE THEIR TIME.

GOD.

YES, BUT SENSELESS MURDERS LIKE THESE KEEP
UNRULY MOBS LIKE THEM IN LINE.

(The mob does the wave.)

FRIAR LAURENCE.

IF YOU ARE GOD,
RELEASE THEM FROM THE CRYPT.

CHORUS.

PRAISE GOD FROM WHOM ALL BLESSINGS OH.

FRIAR LAURENCE.

GO WITH THE FLOW,
REWRITE YOUR DOWNER SCRIPT.

CHORUS.

HE'S GOT A POINT, WHY DON'T YOU
BRING BACK THE KIDS?

GOD.

ARE YOU SOME LUNATIC?
PLEASE, RESURRECTION IS NOT A PARLOR TRICK.

CHORUS.

HALLELUJAH, ATTA BOY, YOU TELL THAT FRIAR.
BE BOP A LU LA, GOD, YOU'RE PREACHING TO THE
CHOIR!

*(**GOD** sits casually center. Everyone else stands
left like a church choir and provides background
vocals.)*

GOD. You know,

>   *(sings)*

>   IT HAS BEEN MENTIONED,
>   AND CERTAINLY MORE THAN ONCE,
>   THE ROAD TO HELL WAS PAVED
>   BY THIS WELL-INTENTIONED BUNCH.

CHORUS.

>   LIKE SERGEANT PEPPER,
>   WE'RE GETTING NEAR THE END.

>   **(CHORUS II** *is 3 voices, usually* **MONTAGUE, LADY CAPULET,** *and* **SAMPSON.** *)*

CHORUS II.

>   THAT'S ALL SHE WROTE. THE CASE IS –

GOD. *(leaping atop the bench)*

>   CLOSETH YOUR EYES.
>   I'VE GOT TO RE-ASCEND.

CHORUS II.

>   SO LONG, GOD.

>   **(GOD** *tries to jump up to the sky.)*

CHORUS.

>   HALLELUJAH, WHOOP DEE DOO, AND HOLY COW!

CHORUS II.

>   THERE'S NO DOUBT.

CHORUS.

>   I AM CONVINCÉD TO GET MY BUTT TO CHURCH RIGHT NOW.
>   HALLELUJAH!

FRIAR LAURENCE.

>   THIS IS A CROCK OF SHIT.[46]

CHORUS.

>   HALLELUJAH! HALLELUJAH, FRIAR, PUT A SOCK IN IT!

>   **(GOD** *laughs like Santa. The* **FRIAR** *ad libs protests.)*

---

46 See Appendix 6 for alternate lyrics and dialogue.

ALL.

HALLELUJAH!

BASSES.

AMEN.

ALL.

HALLELUJAH!

BASSES.

AMEN.

ALL.

HALLELUJAH!
HALLELUJAH, AND AMEN!

(In a matter of seconds, confetti is thrown, **SAMP-SON** *and* **TERRY** *wave pom-poms, and* **LADY CAPULET** *does cheerleader splits. An American flag with John Wayne's face comes out.* **LORD CAPULET** *raises a sign that reads "This was a true story." Blackout.)*

The End

72. BOWS and ENCORE

(Lights up. The cast takes a curtain call to #38, an instrumental of "The Score." Then they sing a reprise of the opening number.)

ENTIRE CAST.

IT'S A BEAUTIFUL DAY IN VERONA!
WE OUGHT TO MAKE THIS TUNE OUR CITY SONG.
IT'S A BEAUTIFUL DAY IN VERONA!
WHAT COULD POSSIBLY GO WRONG?

APPENDIX 1 – ALTERNATE BARNEY SCENES

18. EXT. VILLA CAPULET

(**ROMEO** *and* **BENVOLIO** *are prevented from entering the Capulet house by the* **GATEKEEPER** *from* The Wizard of Oz.)

GATEKEEPER. Orders are...nobody can get into the Capulet party. Not nobody, not no how.

BENVOLIO. But please, it's very important.

ROMEO. And we've got invitations just for the occasion.

GATEKEEPER. There's an occupancy limit. Not nobody, not no how.

(He exits. Sad musical underscore.)

BENVOLIO. Looks like we came a long way for nothing. And I was so happy. I thought I was on my way to the party.

ROMEO. Don't cry, Benvolio. We're going to get you to the party.

(The **GATEKEEPER** *reappears.)*

BENVOLIO. Mercutio was so good to me. And I never appreciated it. Running away and hurting his feelings.

(The **GATEKEEPER** *cries buckets.)*

Now I'll never forgive myself. Never, never, never.

GATEKEEPER. Please don't cry anymore. I'll get you into the Capulet party somehow. I had an Aunt Mercutio myself once.

(He exits.)

ROMEO. You cried so much I thought you were a girl.

BENVOLIO. Shut up, man.

(The "Hello, Drink Up" vamp begins again and they bound into the party.)

27. INT. HALL AT VILLA CAPULET

*(***ROMEO*** and ***JULIET*** sing #10, "Use Each Other Tonight".)*

JULIET.

IF FOR NO OTHER REASON THAT SPITE SO

ROMEO & JULIET.

WHY DON'T WE USE EACH OTHER TONIGHT?

*(The ***GATEKEEPER*** crosses through, keeping an eye on things and enjoying the music.)*

ROMEO.

I'LL GENTLY HOLD YOUR HAND AND DO...LOVEY DOVEY STUFF.

30. EXT. ORCHARD AKA THE BALCONY SCENE

*(***NURSE*** cries and runs away. ***JULIET*** resumes her cadenza in #12.)*

JULIET.

THAT WHICH WE CALL A ROSE—

*(The ***GATEKEEPER*** enters abruptly.)*

GATEKEEPER. Who rang that bell?

JULIET. I'm singing.

GATEKEEPER. Well, that's a horse of a different color.

*(He exits. ***JULIET*** strikes a pose and continues the cadenza.)*

49. INT. JULIET'S CHAMBER – THE NEXT MORNING

(LADY CAPULET enters.)

LADY CAPULET. Juliet, your father and…Ahhh!

(She trades screams with ROMEO.)

Gatekeeper, come quick, it's Romeo Montague!

ROMEO. Don't call for the Gatekeeper. He won't come.

LADY CAPULET. Whatever are you talking about?

ROMEO. It's me, Lady Capulet, the Gatekeeper.

(From offstage, MAN 2 "dubs" ROMEO, so it appears ROMEO is imitating the GATEKEEPER.)

"You don't recognize me because I'm wearing a Romeo mask."

LADY CAPULET. *(#24, continued)* Wow, that's a FANTAS-TIC MASK.

JULIET. That's what I said. But we heard some Montagues infiltrated the party wearing masks and the Gatekeeper here made one in the laboratory.

LADY CAPULET. The laboratory?

ROMEO. Yes, the laboratory. Well, science beckons. Verona, for a while I take my leave.

(Later in Scene 49, CAPULET yells at JULIET.)

CAPULET. …You baggage! You disobedient wretch!

(The NURSE and the GATEKEEPER sneak in and eavesdrop.)

LADY CAPULET. Fie, fie, are you mad?

CAPULET. No. This is mad.

(He goes ballistic.)

I MAKE A DECENT LIVING AT WHATEVER IT IS I DO AND PUT FOOD ON THE TABLE AND ALL I GET FROM YOU IS LIP.

NURSE. He's not even drunk.

CAPULET. I heard that, you old skankbag.

(To **LADY CAPULET***)*

If I'da known this was the kid that was gonna come out of you, I never would have married you.

JULIET. If I would have known you were like this, I would have stayed in.

CAPULET. No more excuses.

LADY CAPULET. Yes, you are looking older by the second.

CAPULET. You are my property and you're going to do as I say.

JULIET. Delay this marriage or make the bridal bed on that dim monument where Tybalt lies.

CAPULET. *(childishly)* Oooh, the suicide threat, I'm soo scared!

(To **NURSE** *and* **GATEKEEPER***)*

Get out of my way or I'll kill you!

(He exits.)

JULIET. Oh, sweet mother, cast me not away.

LADY CAPULET. *(ignoring* **JULIET***)* Hello, Gatekeeper. I'd like to take a tour of your laboratory. Make some masks?

(She touches the **GATEKEEPER***'s staff and makes an enticing exit.)*

GATEKEEPER. Pay no attention to the motion behind that curtain.

(He exits.)

69. INT. THE TOMB

(JULIET is singing #35, "Thank You for Dying First".)

JULIET.

GLAD TO SEE YOU HAVE MY RING
AND MAN, YOU SAID SOME FUNNY THINGS.

(The GATEKEEPER and the NURSE come on from their Scene 30 entrances.)

DON'T EVEN THINK OF INTERRUPTING.

(The GATEKEEPER and the NURSE exit sheepishly and immediately.)

IS THIS A DAGGER
THAT I SEE BEFORE ME?

APPENDIX 2 – CASTING

WOMAN 1 (soprano) plays **JULIET, SAMPSON** (Scenes 2, 41, 54, 71), **ANSELM'S SISTER** (Scene 16), **CORDELIA** (Scene 19), **ASSISTANT APOTHECARY** (Scenes 62-64), and a **BACK UP SINGER** (Scene 64).

WOMAN 2 (mezzo) plays **LADY CAPULET, BALTHAZAR** (Scene 2), the Friar's **PARAMOUR**[1] (Scene 23), **MRS. GIBBS** (Scene 37), **ASSISTANT APOTHECARY** (Scenes 62-64) and a **BACK UP SINGER** (Scene 64).

WOMAN 3 (alto) plays **BENVOLIO, ANSELM'S SISTER** (Scene 16), **SERVING WENCH** (Scenes 27, 28, 48, 53-57), **FRIAR JOHN** (Scenes 32, 50, 53, 70), Terry the **EXECUTIONER** (Scenes 68, 70), a **BACK UP SINGER** (Scene 64), and **ROSALINE** (Scenes 70, 71)[2].

MAN 1 (tenor) plays **ROMEO, ANSELM** (Scene 16), **MICHAELANGELO** (Scene 16), **VICTOR TIRAMISU**[3] (Scene 19), **ANOTHER GUY** in the Chorus (Scenes 41 and 71), and a **BACK UP SINGER** (Scene 64).

MAN 2 (lyric baritone) plays **MERCUTIO, ABRAHAM** (Scene 2), **LORD MONTAGUE** (Scenes 2, 69, 71), **BARNEY/ GATEKEEPER** (Scenes 18, 27, 30, 49, 69), **ANTIPHOLUS** (Scenes 16, 19, 21, 25), **NURSE/FRIAR'S HANDS** (Scene 44)[4], **ANOTHER SERVANT** (Scenes 53-57), the **APOTHECARY** (Scene 62), and a **BACK UP SINGER** (Scene 64).

MAN 3 (tenor) plays **GREGORY, TYBALT**, a **MUSICIAN** (Scene 27), **MR. WEBB** (Scene 37), and a **BACK UP SINGER** (Scene 64).

MAN 4 (tenor) plays **FRIAR LAURENCE, NURSE**, and a **MUSICIAN** (Scene 27).

MAN 5 (tenor-baritone) plays **PRINCE ESCALUS, PARIS**, a **BACK UP SINGER** (Scene 64), and **GOD** (Scene 71).

MAN 6 (bass) plays **LORD CAPULET, GREGORY'S ARM** (Scene 2), the **TOWN CRIER** (Scene 43), a **BACK UP SINGER** (Scene 64), and the guitar (Scenes 45, 61-64)[5].

---

1 Some contend the Friar's Paramour is Lady Capulet, not just another part played by the same actor. If you want to play it that way, that's okay, but then Lord and Lady Capulet cannot dance together in "Use Each Other Tonight."

2 If you want **DA VINCI** to appear for a second (Scene 69), Woman 3 is the only actor available.

3 If you have cast an African-American actor in the play, have him or her play **VICTOR**, AKA Cosby.

4 MAN 3 has also done the hands in some productions.

5 Whoever's able can play guitar, but it is most effective when the **PRINCE** plays guitar on "You Understand."

APPENDIX 3 - COSTUME PLOT

The play is performed in modern dress. At one time, we thought about Mercutio being the only one in a doublet and hose, but the speed and frequency of the changes prohibits it.

The Capulets and the Montagues root for rival sports teams. In Los Angeles, the Capulets were Angels fans and the Montagues were Dodger fans, which informed what Sampson, Abraham, and Balthazar wore, and which determined the color scheme of the wardrobe. Each Capulet had a splash of red and the Montagues all wore something blue.

WOMAN 1. **SAMPSON** wears a baseball hat, a hooded sweatshirt, jeans, and tennis shoes. **JULIET** wears a blouse, perhaps with roses in the pattern, and a rehearsal skirt. **ANSELM'S SISTER** and **CORDELIA** will only have time to drape a long piece of cloth across a downstage shoulder to simulate an evening gown. The **ASSISTANT APOTHECARY** wears a lab coat, sunglasses, and an outré wig. It is nice (but not mandatory) if Woman 1 takes the curtain call as **JULIET**, so that will effect construction of the **SAMPSON** costume.

WOMAN 2. **BALTHAZAR** wears a baseball hat, a baseball jersey, jeans, and tennis shoes. **LADY CAPULET** wears a black mini-skirt, boots, jacket, and probably a red blouse that are so hot you forget she played Balthazar. She wears a boa in "Hello, Drink Up" and she'll need to wear slacks in "Hallelujah". As the **FRIAR'S PARAMOUR**, there is only time to lose the boa, but maybe she could lose the jacket, too, to distinguish her from Lady Capulet. **MRS. GIBBS** wears a knit shawl and glasses. The **ASSISTANT APOTHECARY** wears a lab coat, sunglasses, and an outré wig so she matches Woman 1.

WOMAN 3. **BENVOLIO** wears denim coveralls, a short-sleeved shirt, a tie, and a slouch cap (looking a bit like a member of *Our Gang*). **ANSELM'S SISTER** only has time to drape a piece of cloth over her shoulder to simulate an evening gown. For the **SERVING WENCH,** lose the hat and wear an apron over the coveralls. For **FRIAR JOHN,** wear an bigger than necessary men's brown corduroy sport jacket and a wooden cross that is similar to Friar Laurence's. **TERRY THE EXECUTIONER** wears glasses and a little cardigan sweater over the coveralls. **ROSA-LINE**'s costume is her long hair, which she lets down in Scene 70.

MAN 1. **ROMEO** wears a long-sleeved, blue dress shirt, a tie, and dark trousers. Have duplicate shirts ready for Romeo because the show is a work out for him. **ANSELM** merely uses a cane. **MICHAELANGELO** wears a Halloween-quality Abe Lincoln beard and hat. **VIC-TOR TIRAMISU** wears a floppy, colorful Cosby sweater. **ANOTHER GUY IN THE CHORUS** wears a sport coat that compliments the tie and slacks the actor is already wearing.

MAN 2. **ABRAHAM** wears black trousers, a charcoal grey t-shirt, and a baseball hat. **LORD MONTAGUE** wears a sport coat that goes well with the black trousers and t-shirt (it might have a yachting or club emblem on the left breast). **MERCUTIO** wears an open black dress shirt or long sleeved polo shirt and black trousers. For **BAR-NEY,** emulate the costume from *The Andy Griffith Show* as closely as possible: khaki uniform shirt and trousers, policeman's hat, badge, black gun belt and revolver. If instead your production features the **GATEKEEPER,** emulate the emerald coat and mittens and shako from *The Wizard of Oz.* He also needs a large, false moustache that can be held on by an elastic string. No glue is necessary. **ANTIPHOLUS** appears at Capulet's Fourth of July party. He wears a red, white, and blue vest and/or hat over the grey t-shirt—basically, something simple he can put on and remove a couple of times, so other patriotic accessories are also appropriate. In scene 44, MAN 2 provides a set of **NURSE/FRIAR HANDS**, so he needs a black jacket and a lacy hankie that are duplicates of the **FRIAR/NURSE**'s. **ANOTHER SERVANT** merely wears an apron over the grey t-shirt and the **APOTHECARY** wears a lab coat revealing a bare chest and a wild, David Coverdale-like wig.

MAN 3. **GREGORY** has long hair. He wears an apron over his long peasant shirt. The **TYBALT** costume, a running jacket in Capulet color, is underdressed. **TYBALT** also wears kind of big-framed glasses. In the Fourth of July scene, **TYBALT** attaches some slightly bizarre red, white, and blue pinwheels to his head for the occasion. The **MUSICIAN** in Scene 27 can merely remove the patriotic accoutrements. **MR. WEBB** wears spectacles, a brown vest, and a fedora, since he's right out of *Our Town*. Please note that in Scene 69, the other characters assume Gregory kills himself, but he appears in "Hallelujah!", so he recovers from his injuries. You might want to have a duplicate **GREGORY** costume with a bandage on the belly for that number if it isn't too distracting.

MAN 4 plays **FRIAR LAURENCE**, who wears a black, probably double-breasted suit, black t-shirt, and black shoes. No Roman collar, please. Around his neck on a coarse cord is a wooden cross 6 to 8 inches long. When MAN 4 becomes the **NURSE**, he stows the cross beneath the t-shirt and gestures femininely with a lacy handkerchief. The **FRIAR** wears an Independence Day accessory he can merely remove when he is the **MUSICIAN** in Scene 27.

MAN 5. **PRINCE ESCALUS** wears a politician's suit and tie. **PARIS** has (in previous productions) been a wise guy with a gold necklace, open collar, and blonde wig; a Danny Zuko-like mook in a leather jacket; and a more sensitive person in a lavender sport coat, cravat, and beret. So it is open to interpretation. I like the beret. The cravat can cover the **PRINCE**'s tie. Otherwise, the **PRINCE** has to have a clip-on tie. The ASM has to double for Paris' body, starting in Scene 66, so he or she needs a duplicate outfit, replete with "Don't Tread on Me" flag. **GOD** wears a white choir robe and a stole that is purple or white and gold. When the **PRINCE** imitates Columbo in Scene 51, he wears the classic rumpled grey raincoat.

MAN 6. In Scene 2, MAN 6 is **GREGORY**'s arm for a bit, so he needs a duplicate of **GREGORY**'s left sleeve. **LORD CAPULET** wears a conservative suit that is probably grey with braces and a red tie. Just make it distinguishable from the **PRINCE**'s suit. In the Fourth of July scene, **LORD CAPULET** wears a red sash that says "Happy Fourth of July," and an Uncle Sam top hat. In the Wedding scene, he wears a sash where "Wedding" is crudely written over "Fourth of July". No need for Man 6 to change costume when he's playing the guitar.

APPENDIX 4 – PROPERTIES PLOT

There are a lot of props (the swords and masks not being the least of them) that are, in the tradition of sketch comedy, mimed, or conveyed through object work. Following are the actual items you need.

PROP DESCRIPTION

Rough wooden bench
Stage left, about 1' by 4'. Sturdy enough to stand on. Used for entire show.

Ornate bench
Like one would see in front of a vanity, vaguely Renaissance in design. The top is about 18" by 42". Also stood on and used for entire show.

Red balloon on stick
For Paris as he crosses through in **Scene 12**.

Harmonica, key of D
For the Prince in **Scene 14**.

Scepter or drum major's baton
For Lord Capulet, starting in **Scene 16**.

Fourth of July accessories
Flags or hats that can be hidden on one's person, **Scene 16**

Cane
For Anselm's cross through, **Scene 16**.

Boa
Lady Capulet, **Scene 16**.

Red, White & Blue hat
Capulet puts it on Juliet in **Scene 16**.

Bunting
Michaelangelo holds it beneath himself when he appears.

Flag
Revolutionary War flag with 13 stars that Romeo and Benvolio manipulate in **Scene 16**. Also used in "It's a Beautiful Day for a Wedding" and "Hallelujah".

Holster and revolver
Part of Barney's costume for **Scene 18**. It might be really funny if he drew the gun in a panic in **Scene 30**.

Staff
If the production uses the Gatekeeper, he needs a staff, such as a Beefeater would use, that is 5 to 6 feet long. (In The *Wizard of Oz*, the character wields a rifle with a flower in it, but it read inappropriately for the show.)

Spray bottle
For the Gatekeeper's tears.

Claves
For Musician in **Scene 27**.

Egg
For Musician in **Scene 27**.

Stuffed bear 1
AKA Leonard, introduced by Mercutio in **Scene 29**. Also used by Lord Capulet in **Scene 69**.

Stuffed bear 2
A duplicate attached to a black stick or dowel (operated by cast member or stagehand) so Leonard can enter and exit on his own power in **Scene 38.**

Guitar
To accompany "You Understand" and "The Score".

Notepad
For Prince's Columbo, **Scene 51.**

Cigar
For Prince's Columbo, **Scene 51**.

Flowers
For Gregory, first used in **Scene 53**. Have four or five duplicate sets of flowers ready. They ought to be a large bouquet of carnations or gladiolas.

Flag
For Serving Wench, first used in **Scene 53**. Revolutionary War's "Don't Tread on Me" with the snake. You need a duplicate flag for Paris' body double.

Book
For Lady Capulet in **Scene 55**. It is textbook sized and is clearly titled *Faking It.*

Brochure
A triptych brochure of a convent that Friar gives Juliet in **Scene 67**.

Copy of The Watchtower
Friar enters with this magazine and tosses it aside in **Scene 69.**

Noose
Flies in above stage right bench in **Scene 71.**

Wind instrument
For God in **Scene 71.** A trombone, a saxophone, and a sousaphone have all been used.

Razor scooter
For God in **Scene 71** if there are no stairs in the audience for him to descend.

Pom poms

For women in **Scene 71,** concealed in the sleeves of God's robe or velcroed to the wooden bench.

Flag

For Scene 71. American Flag with John Wayne's face on it, concealing on Another Guy in Chorus' person, displayed by him and the Friar. Flag with 13 Stars is displayed by Gregory and Lord Montague.

Confetti

Concealed in the pockets of the actors and thrown in **Scene 71.**

Sign

For Lord Capulet in **Scene 71**. It reads "This Was a True Story."

APPENDIX 5 - GROUNDPLAN

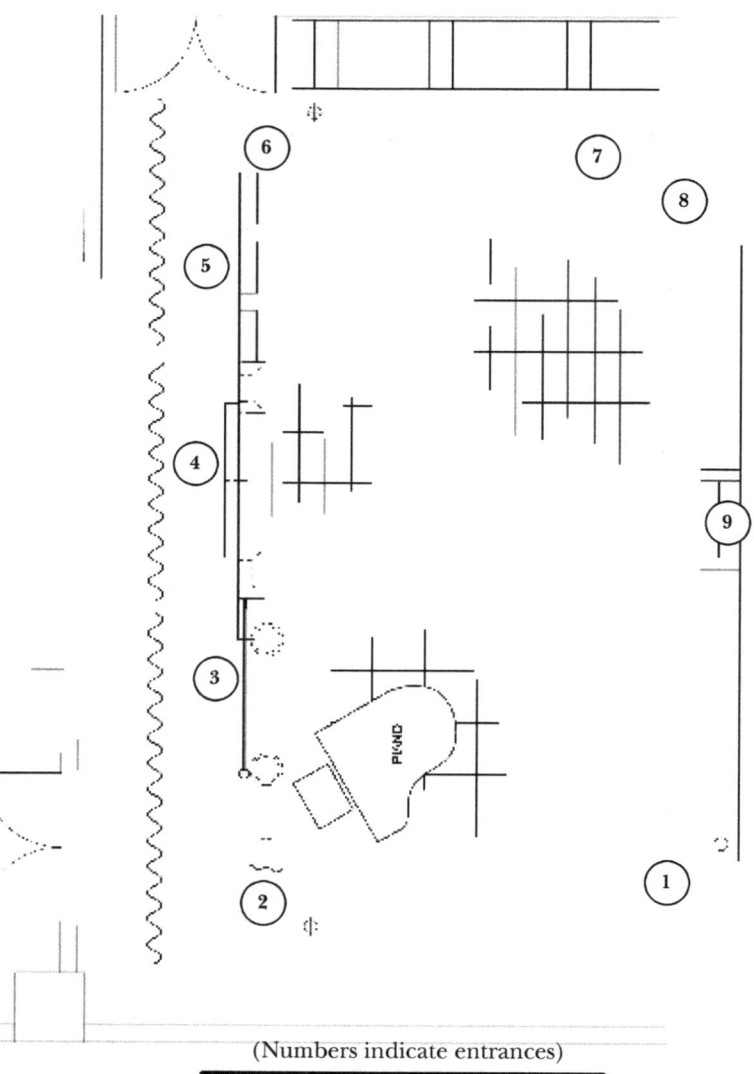

(Numbers indicate entrances)

CHICAGO SHAKESPEARE STUDIO THEATER	
THE PEOPLE VS. FRIAR	
SCENIC & LIGHT DESIGN: H. GRAFF & R. PETERSON	
DIRECTOR: R. WEST	PSM: J. COLLINS
GROUND PLAN	
SCALE: 1/4" = 1'-0"	DATE: **4/11//04**

APPENDIX 6 - ALTERNATE LANGUAGE

If you're reading this, you got as far as page 10 in the script and said, "I want to produce *Friar Laurence* but I can't because of all the swearing. Shit!" Fear not. Below are author-approved alternate lyrics and dialogue.

1. Scene 2, page 8.

Change to:
WE ARE OFTEN NAUSEOUS AND CRANKY

2. Scene 2, page 9.

Change to:
AS STUPID MACHO LOUTS,
WE LIKE PREYING ON THE WEAK.
TO INSULT EACH OTHER'S MANHOOD,
WE CALL EACH OTHER "GEEK."

3. Scene 2, page 10.

Change to:
WHERE WE COME FROM, THE SKULLS ARE NUMB.

4. Scene 2, page 11.

Change to:
WHO GIVES A HOOT ABOUT THE POOR
OR DOING VOLUNTEER WORK!?

5. Scene 2, page 13.

Change to:
FRIAR LAURENCE.
AND THEN THAT SILLY PRINCE APPEARED–
OH, DEAR, WHAT AM I DOIN'?

6. Scene 6, page 19.

Change to:
BENVOLIO. Hey, there's loose women and free booze down the street.

7. Scene 6, page 20.

Change to:

CAPULET. Wow. He's moving like someone told him there's loose women and free booze.

8. Scene 7, page 21.

Change to:

I'LL RUN OFF WITH A SERVANT TO EMBARRASS
("I'll" comes on the end of 4 n measure 3. "Run" becomes the downbeat in measure 4.)

9. Scene 8, pages 24-25.

Change to:

BENVOLIO.
JUST SEE OTHER PEOPLE
BREAK OUT OF YOUR SHELL.
ROMEO.
YOU CALLED ME A CHICKEN!
BENOVLIO.
I MEAN YOU'RE COMPELLED
TO FIND A NEW FILLY.
ROMEO.
PLACE A BET ON A HORSE?
BENVOLIO.
MUST I SPELL IT OUT
IN A CODE THAT IS MORSE?
ROMEO. Yes, please.
BENVOLIO. Look, take this time to play the field.
ROMEO. Okay, but I want to play shortstop.
BENVOLIO. Aargh!

(sings again)

FIND MISTRESS QUICKLY
AND QUIT BELLY-ACHING.

ROMEO.
YOUR MIXED METAPHORS
ARE MERCUTIO'S MAKING.
BENVOLIO.
JUST SEE OTHER PEOPLE
YOU'RE YOUNG, RICH, AND BLESSED.
YOU"RE A PAIN IN THE NECK.

10. Scene 10, page 26.

Change to:

CAPULET. *(To* **GREGORY***)* It's a Fourth of July party. Where's your Italian patriotism? Hi, Friar.

11. Scene 10, page 27.

Change to:

FRIAR LAURENCE.
I MEAN GO GET JIGGY.
I MEAN YOU GET DOWN.
YOU CAN RESCUE A DAMSEL
WHO'S ON THE REBOUND.
ROMEO & BENVOLIO.
THIS MAN OF THE CLOTH BEARS
NO NAIVETÉ.

12. Scene 10, pages 27-28.

Change to:

ROMEO, BENVOLIO & FRIAR.
SEE OTHER PEOPLE.
BENVOLIO.
'CAUSE SHE'S IN A CLOISTER.
FRIAR LAURENCE.
THERE'S FISH IN THE OCEAN.
BENVOLIO.
THE WORLD IS YOUR OYSTER!

13. Scene 12, page 30.

Change to:

(**JULIET** *flops down on the bench.*)

JULIET. I hate everything.

NURSE. *(Chuckling)* I can't help but think of my late husband.

JULIET. He hated everything, too?

NURSE. When you were a little girl, you bumped your head and fell on your face. My late husband Jerry said, "Be cheerful, wipe thine eyes. Some falls are means the happier to arise."

JULIET. That didn't help then and it definitely doesn't help now.

NURSE. You can really tell this is a wig?

JULIET. Yes, I can tell it's a wig, now get out.

NURSE. Juliet, what's wrong with you?

JULIET. I don't want to marry Paris.

NURSE. Juliet, you mustn't say such things.

(**LADY CAPULET** *enters.*)

Lady Capulet, Juliet says she doesn't want to marry Paris.

LADY CAPULET. Oh, I know, sweetheart, you're frightened. You're just a little girl.

(*The* **NURSE** *chuckles at a fond memory.*)

What's so funny?

NURSE. I can't help but recall my late husband Jerry saying, "Oh, mother dear, we're not the fortunate ones, and girls just wanna have fun."

14. Scene 12, page 32.

Change to:

NURSE.

HIS HABITS WILL BECOME ENCHANTING
WHEN HE'S WATCHING SPORTS AND RANTING.

15. Scene 12, page 32.

Change to:

JULIET.
NO MORE ADVICE!
THANK YOU ALL FOR TRYING
BUT I'M DIFFERENT THAN YOU HAGS.
I'VE GOT BRAINS AND LOOKS

16. Scene 13, page 34.

Change to:

AND I'VE GOT BICEPS LIKE KING KONG.

17. Scene 13, page 34.

Change to:

I'VE NOT CLIMBED A MOUNTAIN TOO STEEP.

18. Scene 15, page 37.

Change to:

ROMEO. Gimme a break.

19. Scene 23 & 24, page 48.

Cut 23 & 24 and condense as follows:

22. INT. DUNGEON

PRINCE. So now you took it upon yourself to introduce Romeo and Juliet…to foment disaster.

FRIAR LAURENCE. Oh, come on, Prince, you know that didn't happen.

(Lights change. to….)

25. INT. HALL AT VILLA CAPULET

*(The cast ad libs party chatter for 8 beats. Everyone freezes when **ROMEO** and **JULIET** spot one another across the room. They run to each other.)*

ROMEO. If I profane with my unworthiest hand this holy shrine, the gentle sin is this, my lips, two blushing pilgrims –

(**JULIET** *lays a most audacious kiss on him.*)

Wowzer.

(**ROMEO** *and* **JULIET** *freeze, too. Lights change.*)

26. INT. DUNGEON

FRIAR LAURENCE. No, no, it wasn't like that either.

PRINCE. Yes, I know enough about physics to know that people just don't freeze.

FRIAR LAURENCE. The meeting of Romeo and Juliet was far more ordinary.

(*All reanimate as lights change.*)

20. Scene 27, page 50.

Change to:

SERVING WENCH. We're out of the merlot. The bathroom is over there. Yes, I have a boyfriend.

ROMEO. Thank you, but that isn't my question.

SERVING WENCH. *(About to crack)* I'm just a temp!

ROMEO. Okay, okay, what lady's that which doth enrich the hand of yonder knight?

SERVING WENCH. I don't know. But I hear she's easy.

21. Scene 27, page 51.

Change to:

JULIET.
I'LL SCRATCH YOUR BACK
ROMEO.
AND I'LL SCRATCH YOURS.

22. Scene 30, page 56.

Change to:

(**NURSE** *enters. Note: the following italicized dialogue ought to be changed as current events dictate. One might choose a TV character, such as* Saved by the Bell*'s Mr. Belding, or a public figure, like Mayor/Boyfriend Antonio Villaraigosa. But, honestly, this is probably the place where a high school cast ought to insert the name of their principal.*)

23. Scene 31, pages 58-59.

Change to:

FRIAR LAURENCE. When he came to me the next morning, he was very sincere, yet euphoric. Down to earth, yet totally wack.

PRINCE. This is where it gets complex.

FRIAR LAURENCE. And complicated. I was picking flowers...

24. Scene 32, page 61.

Change to:

FRIAR LAURENCE. Holy hell!

25. Scene 33, page 62.

Change to:

PRINCE. I wish you'd have been my priest. My wife and I had to meet with other couples for three whole months.

26. Scene 37, page 67.

Change to:

ROMEO. I wanted to have sex. Why do I have to get married at all? Listen, Ma, for the last time I ask you.

27. Scene 37, page 68.

Change to:

(ROMEO kisses JULIET in a way that makes the audience cheer. MR. WEBB reacts benignly, as if nothing is out of the ordinary.)

28. Scene 38, page 69.

Change to:

TYBALT. Thou consort'st with Romeo.

MERCUTIO. Consort?

TYBALT. Associate, keep company, socialize, hang out.

MERCUTIO. I know what it means! 'Zounds, consort!

29. Scene 39, page 71.

Change to:

FRIAR. And for no reason!

30. Scene 46, page 86.

Change to:

(They dance but stop to say the name of each couple. Current events will dictate the replacement of the couples' names. Here's a few examples for 2010 high school students.)

ROMEO. We're like Edward and Bella.

JULIET. We're like Zach and Vanessa.

ROMEO. We're like Taylor Swift and five guys I know personally.

31. Scene 50, page 93.

Change to:

JULIET. You block! You stone! You worse than senseless thing! Come up with a solution or I'll kill myself.

32. Scene 51, pages 96-97.

Change to:

*(The **FRIAR** is seated as before. The **PRINCE**, imitating David Caruso's Horatio Caine, enters. He wears his suit without the tie. He might wear a red wig. But most importantly, he makes dramatic use of his sunglasses.)*

PRINCE. Verona has a new breed of criminal. You.

FRIAR LAURENCE. Can I help you with something?

PRINCE. Yes. Because you've got something to hide.

FRIAR LAURENCE. I've got nothing to hide. You've got the wrong man, clearly.

PRINCE. Then you'll want to clear this up. You gave a fourteen year old girl a speedball. First you marry her and then you give her a speedball. Isn't that what happened?

FRIAR LAURENCE. Prince, what the hell are you doing?

PRINCE. Okay, you did the whole *Our Town* thing.

*(The **PRINCE** runs off in a hissy huff.)*

33. Scene 53, pages 98-99.

Change to:

LADY CAPULET.

YOU'VE GOT TO TELL HER ABOUT HER DUTY

YOU KNOW THE STUFF ABOUT THE BIRDS AND THE
    BEES.

YOU KNOW THE HONEYMOON IN THE BEDROOM.

SHE OUGHTA OPERATE WITH SOME EXPERTISE.

NURSE.

I'M PRETTY SURE JULIET ALREADY KNOWS.

LADY CAPULET.

MEN ARE PIGS AND SHE MUST BE ON HER GUARD.

YOU BREAST FED HER SO YOU KNOW BETTER.

I JUST SIGN HER REPORT CARD.

NURSE.

NOT ME, YOU TELL HER. I'M JUST A SERVANT,

LADY CAPULET.

BUT IT'S KINDA LIKE YOU'RE ONE OF HER FRIENDS.

(From every available entrance, hands clap four times.)

LADY CAPULET.

TO DISAPPOINT HIM IS DISHONOR.

NURSE.

I JUST BRUSH HER HAIR AND TRIM THE SPLIT ENDS.

LADY CAPULET.

YOU'VE GOT TO TELL HER.

NURSE.

NOT ME, YOU TELL HER.

BOTH.

TELL HER SO SHE'LL KNOW WHAT TO DO!

34. Scene 55, page 102.

Change to:

CAPULET.

DAMN IT! PUT THE FLOWERS OVER THERE!

35. Scene 57, page 103.

Change to:

CAPULET.

PUT THE FLOWERS OVER THERE, BE DAMNED!

36. Scene 58, page 104.

Change to:

O WOE, O DREADFUL FRIGGING WOE.

37. Scene 60, page 107.

Change to:

CAPULET. Gregory, go to the houses of all the guests and tell them it's not a wedding, it's a funeral... and put those feathermucking flowers over there!

38. Scene 63, page 109.

Change to:

FRIAR LAURENCE.
THEN FLASH YOUR BLASTED CLERGY BADGE.
IT GETS YOU INTO ANY SCENE.

39. Scene 64, page 111.

Change to:

FRIAR LAURENCE.
MAYBE IT'S JUST COINCIDENCE
OR A SERIES OF RANDOM EVENTS.
BUT IT ALL HIT THE FAN
AND GUESS WHO'S THE FAN.

40. Scene 65, page 114.

Change to:

PARIS. You call that a stab?

(**ROMEO** *throws a dagger at him.* **PARIS** *makes an SFX so we know it hits the mark.*)

Oh boy, I hope I don't fall on that.

Oh no, oh no. Sonuva–

41. Scene 65, page 115.

Change to:

ROMEO. *(cont.)*

THANK YOU FOR DYING—

(Spoken as it suddenly hits him)

Damn, Gary, this is strong stuff.

42. Scene 67, page 116.

Change to:

FRIAR LAURENCE. Hello? Hello? Is someone in the mausoleum…*(sees* **ROMEO***)* What the hell! Romeo! How did you get here so fast? I live next door! You came all the way from Mantua! What do I pay that security company for? *(sees* **PARIS***)* Double what the hell!

*(***JULIET*** wakes up.)*

JULIET. Oh comfortable Friar!

FRIAR LAURENCE. Triple what the hell!

43. Scene 70, page 124.

Change to:

FRIAR LAURENCE. I know this has been said before but those masks are fantastic.

44. Scene 70, page 124.

Change to:

ROSALINE. That's right, loser.

45. Scene 71, page 125.

Change to:

CAN WE JUST GOOF AROUND 'TIL THE END?

46. Scene 72, page 128.

Change to:

FRIAR LAURENCE.

I'M SURE THIS IS A CROCK.

CHORUS.

HALLELUJAH! HALLELUJAH, YOU'RE SCISSORS, HE'S A
ROCK!

OTHER TITLES AVAILABLE FROM SAMUEL FRENCH

HAMLET II (BETTER THAN THE ORIGINAL!)

Sam Bobrick, original story by William Shakespeare

Comedy / 11m, 2f (doubling possible) / Simple Set

Hamlet II is a mad, zany parody of the original with a much happier ending. Rosencrantz and Guildenstern come off like Groucho Marx, Ophelia is a loose woman and alas, poor Yorick is turned into a crazy comic. Then there's Gertrude, Claudius, Laertes and the old dead King as you've never seen them before. And what does Prince Hamlet think of this new approach to his life? He loves it and why not? To catch the conscience of the king, he gets to write a hit musical. Also included are the loves, hates, sword fights, poetry, religion, treachery and deceit that go with the territory as well as occasional stabs at the meaning of life.

OEDIPUS FOR KIDS!

Book by Gil Varod and Kimberly Patterson
Lyrics by Gil Varod
Music and additional material by Robert J. Saferstein

2m 1f / Musical Comedy / Unit set

Unfolding in real-time, *Oedipus for Kids!* turns the audience into attendees of the latest performance of the Fuzzy Duck Theatre Company, a three-person troupe dedicated to performing the classics for children. Having had success with previous offerings such as *Uncle Tommy's Cabin*, company founder Alistair has decided that the next logical step is tackling Sophocles' *Oedipus Rex* with songs such as "What's It Like When Ya Get The Plague?" and "A Little Complex." But all is not as pleasant as it seems with the Fuzzy Ducks: Alistair is in the middle of a bitter divorce with troupe member Catalina, who suspects something is up when she learns that tonight's audience includes the executives from sponsor Beanz! Coffee for Kids. Evan, the third troupe member, is a newly-trained recent hire with questionable acting methods. He uses these to play Oeddy, "a little boy a lot like you," who runs away from home when he finds out that he is destined to do something terrible to his Mommy and Daddy.

Please note: this play is not for young audiences.

"A spoof of children's theater, with some truly funny songs and endearingly loopy performances from a cast of just three."
– Charles Isherwood, *The New York Times*

"This twisted treat lives up to its outrageous title admirably. Patterson and Varod's book captures a Christopher Durang-like sensibility that is infectiously entertaining. Varod and Saferstein's score is a total treat, too (which I've been humming more than a few times). Yes, you can do *Oedipus for Kids!* and it can be just as horrifyingly fun as it sounds."
– Joe Tropia, *Broadway.com*